Evod and the Children of the Star

Laya Brandt

ISBN: 978-1-952661-70-9

Endorsements

Laya Brandt has captured the essence of the Gospel in an adventure story that will encourage young people to follow the Holy Spirit. It's a clear message that will touch the hearts of even adults who read it.

From Faye Higbee, Author of <u>Dog Paw Chronicles</u> , <u>Whispers of Heaven,</u> <u>Bobby Convict</u>
BITTEROOT MOUNTAIN PUBLISHING HOUSE

—————————————

Enjoyed reading Evod and the Children of the Star. Some of the mysteries remind me of something author Jonathan Cahn would share.

From Ginny Seymour, - Publisher Evensong Publishing
Author of The Covenant Curriculum
<u>The Whistle Hollar Toads Makin Music</u>
EVENSONG PUBLISHING

CHAPTER ONE
EVOD

"What is the least common factor of 36?"

Who cares? David Roth shrugged and slouched in his chair. He kept his eyes on his fifth -grade teacher as he reached into his desk and found his library book about the knights of the Round Table. He opened it and eased it halfway out of his desk. He read a few lines before the thud of a book dropping on the floor nearby interrupted him. David shoved the book back into his desk.

The warm, stale air threatened to lull David to sleep. As his head dipped below his propped hand, he heard a faint tapping at the back of the room. He ignored it and tried to stay awake.

The noise grew louder and louder, until David could not ignore it any longer. He thought the second--floor window might break, so he turned himself sideways to look at the source of the racket.

A bird, a giant bird the size of his desk with clear, shimmering wings hovered outside the classroom window. How was that possible?

David rubbed his eyes. Maybe he'd fallen asleep

and it was all a dream. A bird whose wings didn't flap A bird with glimmering iridescent wings? Iridescent, last week's spelling word had stuck to him like gum to the bottom of his shoe. He'd never heard of a bird with wings like that before.

David glanced at his book and scanned a few lines. Nope, no birds there. The hitch in Miss Hansen's voice drew David's attention. Had she seen the bird? Her cursor moved down the board as the students reviewed the times table. He peeked over his shoulder. The bird rammed his beak against the glass in quick movements. David's cheeks burned. He slunk further in his chair and pulled up the collar of his uniform. His heart thumped against his chest. "David." David jerked around.

"Come out, come out. You can be free with me, David."

David spun back toward Miss Hansen. His eyes wide. He swallowed. How did the   bird know his name?

"David, I'll show you what you need to learn. Come out."

"Five!"

"Seven!"

David gulped, and then pinched the inside of his arm. "Nine!"

David surveyed the room to see if he was the only one that even noticed the bird. His classmates followed the lesson. Some called out answers, and others wiggled in their chairs as they raised their hands.

Again, he was alone, different from everyone else. The others already made fun of him for reading instead of playing video games. This would be no different. He didn't fit in. "Four times what equals what?" David rolled his eyes.

Slowly, David looked around the room. He noticed the new girl, Julia, wasn't paying attention to the teacher either. She was twirling one of her braids

and chewing gum loudly. With each smack, she twirled faster. She was staring out the same window. Did she see the bird?

Suddenly, she froze, turned toward David and gaped at him with eyes wide and the wad of gum clearly visible inside her mouth. David's face mirrored her own. Unable to speak or react, he watched as Julia slowly got up and strode towards the window. It looked like she was going to let the bird in.

David sprang from his seat and stepped in front of her.

"What are you doing?" he whispered loudly.

"It's a dove-" Julia said quietly. "It wants us to come out and be free. It wants to teach us something."

David's stomach jumped.

"How do you know what it wants?"

"It told me." Julia's voice was as calm as the bird's expression.

Whoa! She could hear the bird too. "Okay, but don't let it in." He stepped back as Julia lifted the latch. The old metal squealed as the bird flew slightly backwards. David looked around at his classmates. They all seemed to be in a trance. Their eyes were glued to the back of Miss Hansen's head, and they were reciting numbers in a droning monotone. David started back to his seat, but Julia grabbed his wrist and silently shook her head. She pointed towards the window.

David pulled back, and his mind raced with all the possibilities lurking outside the window: *We could get caught by Miss Hansen, then what? We could fall! That would be some serious head damage. OR the bird could attack us and carry us away!*

David examined Julia from head to toe. She looked very skinny and scruffy, but unafraid. She appeared to have enough courage to go outside.

He and Julia peered at the ledge outside the window. David gulped when he looked down. The ground was far below. He decided to take a chance and find out what the bird wanted. David closed his eyes and whispered to Julia, "You first."

"Okay, it's easy." Her voice was cheerful and worry-free. She stepped through the open window and stood on the ledge. David slowly and carefully followed.

A stately red oak stood outside the window. Its russet leaves formed a cloak over its gnarled old branches. The tree was sturdy enough to hold them, but how could they reach the branches which were clearly a few feet away from the window?

"What now?" Julia asked as she looked at David. He shrugged, secretly hoping that was the end of their "adventure".

The bird slowly circled the tree and then flew up and rested on its top, like a star on a Christmas tree. David watched, now in awe. Then the tree branches began to move. One of them stretched over to them in a fluid movement.

"Wow, did you see that?" Julia studied the branch. "I'm gonna touch it."

She leaned over. "It feels warm and soft like my mom. I think I'll trust it." She let go of the ledge and grabbed onto the branch. It cradled her, then gracefully lowered her to the ground.

A second branch reached out to David. He hesitated. The twigs at the end of the branch formed a hand and tilted up at him. The "pointer finger" twitched forward, beckoning him to come. David almost let out a full laugh but reminded himself of the classroom with its window ajar. He reached out and grabbed the branch. It brought him down quickly in a sweep that both surprised and delighted him.

That was fun!

On the ground now, David and Julia looked around for anyone nearby who could have spied their escape. No one was in the yard outside the school. The rich manicured lawns were empty except for David, Julia and the bird.

Julia turned to David. "Do you believe this?"

David smiled and shook his head. "Not really – not yet."

CHAPTER TWO
THE TENT AND THE WHIRLWIND

The bird took off from the treetop. Filled with sudden energy, as if by magic, the children ran after it. The bird looped-de-looped and did a figure eight in the air above their heads, making it easy to keep up. As they ran, David noticed they were going very fast, faster than usual. The scenery sped by as if they were in a car. No feeling of shoe on grass or pebble. "We're not on the ground anymore!" David exclaimed.

"We're flying! Look!" Julia stuck her right foot out in front, then her left. She giggled. "This is crazy!"

"It is crazy." David waved his arms. He lost his balance for a second but was able to concentrate and right himself. David laughed and turned towards Julia. "... I feel like I've been here before."

"You mean that feeling you've been somewhere before but you know you haven't?" David nodded.

"I don't know what's going on but one thing I do know- this is better than being stuck in that room!"

"It sure is!"

The bird slowed down and lowered itself into a

field. David and Julia were able to slow down too. When they steadied themselves, and stopped laughing, Julia whispered, "Ssh, it's stopping in that bush. Let's stop too."

Above David and Julia, a blue sky with fluffy clouds rested peacefully. Emerald grass and shrubbery surrounded them. A slight breeze was in the air.

"This feels like another country, David."

"I know, but I feel safe here. Like we won't be discovered. For some reason knowing that bird is here makes me feel safe." David pointed behind them and they both looked at their school, barely a gray shadow on the distant horizon.

David continued to look around, and now he saw a huge purple tent to his right! Golden ropes held the tent pegs, and the wind fluttered blue, white and purple panels of cloth. "Where did that tent come from? I didn't see it before!"

"Me, neither. What's it doing here?"

"I sure don't know."

"Do you hear that music?" Julia hopped up and down. "Let's go in."

He put up his hand. "We'd better not. We don't know what it is, or who it belongs to." -Julia crept closer. She stopped and held her hand to her ear. She put her other hand behind her back, holding up a finger to silence David as she gazed into the tent. From the bush, the bird swooped down over their heads and entered the tent. A brilliant light came from within. It temporarily blinded David.

"Julia, where are you?" David shielded his eyes. "Julia, the light is too bright."– "I know, but I just have to know what's in there. I can't see anything." Julia craned her neck and crawled forward on the grass.

"Let's just wait here, Julia. I feel like we're not supposed to go in."

"Why not?" Julia snapped. "Come on." Julia watched David, but when he didn't follow her, she went back and sat next to him. "You're no fun!"

Before David could defend himself, the bird emerged with a scroll in its beak. It circled above David and Julia's heads three times and went back to the bush. Then it cooed and dropped the scroll. A huge funnel cloud sprang up from the ground where the scroll had landed. The bird flew into the cloud and so did the tent. David and Julia scrambled to their feet and held on to each other.

"What are we doing here?" David moaned. "We shouldn't have left school." "It's too late now!" Julia screamed over the rushing sound.

The whirlwind moved over the ground in a straight line. It cut a swath in front of them, causing all the trees in its path to turn black.

"I think it's a tornado." David cried out. "We should take cover."

"Where? There's no place to go." Julia looked down at her feet. "Let's try to stand still."

Plants, then shrubs, then small trees were sucked into the funnel cloud and then popped out again. The funnel became dark and foreboding. It moved inch-by-inch, foot-by-foot, yard-by yard.

David turned to run, but Julia grabbed his arm.

"No, David. We can't outrun a tornado! Let's see what happens first." Julia let go of David. "It doesn't seem to be headed this way. It's going in a straight line, back and forth." She waved her arm in front of her. "I think we'll have plenty of time to get out of its way."

"I hope you're right."

The funnel passed a few feet across from them, but by then they were frozen in fright. They felt a harsh wind rustle across their faces, and their hair stirred.

David was happy when the funnel cloud moved out of the field. "That was close," he said. "Now it's out of sight." David's shoulders lowered, and he sank down on the grass.

Julia remained standing. "It left half of the field black. The part where we are hasn't been touched- it's still bright, full and green.

"I know," David said. "What just happened?

"I don't know. It's almost like it MEANT to miss us."

"I'm sure glad." David sighed. "That was more than scary."

CHAPTER THREE
THE CHOICE

David pressed his palms against his legs and tried to slow his breathing. He looked down at the ground.

"The dove is back, David!"

David stood up. "I'm not so sure it's a dove."

"Of course, it is, David. Look at those white feathers and big eyes."

"Well…I guess you could be right, Julia. We can call it a dove for now."

The dove's eyes locked into theirs. David could read its mind again and it said, "Choose."

"Choose what?" David asked out loud.

Julia looked shocked as she turned to face David. "You heard that?"

"Yeah, I guess I did." David smiled at her. Then he looked up. "Okay," he said to the dove, "No problem, we choose this green side," he pointed to his feet, "not the black side of the field."

"That's right! Who would want to go over there?"

"*Choose,*" the bird repeated and flew off into the middle of the blackness. It pecked at the ground, and a treasure chest came up, like a plant breaking forth in time-lapse photography. The children gasped. The chest opened, revealing dozens of sparkling jewels, in a multitude of colors. David and Julia's hearts leapt within them.

"I can't believe it. Look at all that stuff. Why, there must be a hundred gems in that box, Julia."

"I know, we will be rich." She clasped her hands together.

"Whose are they? Is the dove giving them to us?" David turned excitedly to his companion. "Man, Julia, this adventure, even if we get punished for leaving the classroom, is going to be worth it." David pictured himself shoving handfuls of jewels into his pockets.

Julia was the first to take off toward the treasure chest. "NO!" the dove shouted in David's thoughts.

She slowed down, took another step, then stopped. "Some kind of strange feeling is coming over me!" She rested her palm on her chest and stared at David. "It's like that dark funnel cloud is in my chest, where my heart is. I don't like this creepy feeling. It's nothing like the fun of following the dove. David, we can't go in there. Something's not right."

"What do you mean?" He quickly ran a few steps toward the treasure chest. He too stopped in his tracks. "Something's not right. I feel weird too. It's like a cold wind is pushing against my body." He frowned and looked at Julia. "I can't go any further either. What's going on? I thought we were gonna be rich. Now I don't even want to have this stuff. This is creepy."

The dove flew overhead. They looked up. It cooed and swooped in the opposite direction. It seemed to be smiling.

Can a dove smile? Or think? David gazed upward. It appeared that way. Julia heard it talk, too. And it knows what we are doing.

He looked over at Julia. Her head tilted back, she had a smile on her face. "Maybe we should follow it." he yelled over his shoulder as he took off running.

"Okay!" Julia was right behind him.

CHAPTER FOUR
THE CAVE

They followed the dove to an entrance of a large cave and anxiousness rose in David's chest. The dove flew right in, -and Julia rushed after him.

"What an adventure. I see a path." Her voice echoed from the cave. "Come on, David!"

"We don't know if it's safe, Julia," he yelled. Julia ignored him. His chest got tighter. Her voice bounced off the cave walls and echoed back to him. "Look at that waterfall up ahead."

Waterfall? He had to see this. He wouldn't go too far.

The whooshing sound of water pouring over rocks lured him. He peered inside and saw light reflecting and flickering off some rocks deep in the cave. David's chest released and fluttered with excitement as he started into the cave.

Sure enough, as David traveled further in, he found a path leading downward toward a beautiful crystal-clear waterfall. Behind the cascading water, a rainbow of colored stones sparkled out at him. He stopped next to Julia and gazed in wonder. When he did, he heard beautiful singing in blended tones, like a choir. David turned to Julia and said, "Can you hear that?"

She nodded. I can't understand the words, but it makes me feel peaceful inside." "Me too."

At that moment, a gust of wind surged above them. The dove hovered over their heads. They lifted their eyes, but all they could see was a pair of expansive wings highlighted in gleaming white light. Gradually the light overcame the darkness in the cave, revealing the brilliant blue eyes of their new companion.

"The dove isn't singing Julia, but it definitely wanted us to come to this beautiful place."

"I- I know." Julia's voice echoed off the cave walls as she addressed the dove. What is your name?" Julia asked.

"Evod." the dove gently replied.

Julia exhaled. "David, did you hear that?"

"I sure did. What a beautiful name- Evod."

David and Julia stood in awe for a long time.

Finally, the dove turned and flew a few feet deeper into the cave. It stopped and perched on an outcropping of rocks. It seemed to wait for them.

"Let's see where else Evod will lead us." Julia whispered.

"Okay." David's body tingled.

David and Julia walked to where the dove awaited. It lifted off slowly as its enormous wings spread like a canopy across the width of the cave. The children walked underneath, glancing at each other.

"Do you believe this?" mouthed Julia.

David shook his head and smiled.

Evod swiftly flew up ahead. David and Julia followed, hesitantly at first, but increasing in speed, indicating their anticipation. They crested a small hill, and the dirt beneath them gave way. Julia shrieked.

"We're going to die." David tumbled into a cavern that glowed from a huge fire in the center. David and Julia looked, spellbound, deep into its captivating flames.

"Where are we?" Julia asked.

"I don't know...some kind of underground cave..., how do we get out?"

"Get out? I don't want to get out. This is way cool."

David realized he was worrying again. Why did he say that? Julia's right - This is way cool. He might as well just look around. "Yeah, it is pretty cool." He discovered the fire was surrounded by a circle of rocks, then a circle of grass. That is where they were lying. The grass was the softest grass he had ever felt. Dancing shadows reflected off the multicolored stones that were inlaid in the high walls.

Julia sighed and stretched her arms over her head. "I feel like I could stay in this place forever. I feel peaceful and happy and most of all, loved somehow."

"That's funny, so do I, right now. It's very peaceful... but, where's the dove? Do you see it anywhere?"

"No, I still can't figure out where we are."

David looked around, feeling unsettled by the disappearance of Evod.

All at once the cave's far wall opened and a set

of stairs descended. David and Julia couldn't see what was at the top of the stairs- it was obscured by some type of fog. They looked at each other.

"Look at that, David. Should we go up?"

"OK," David whispered. He didn't want to seem like a coward to Julia.

They snaked their way around the fire, careful not to breach the rock border, on their way to the stairs. When they got to the bottom step, fear embraced them.

"You first," said Julia.

"No, you," choked out David.

Evod cooed gently over them,-and they looked up. Its eyes were gleaming peace again.

"We trusted this dove before. Let's trust it again," said Julia.

"OK, uh-er, of course." David agreed in his heart even before his lips spoke the words. Up the stairs they went and at the top, they found a door. Opening it cautiously, he was shocked to find they were rising out of the basement of the school.

"We're in the school, David! The first floor."

"I know, this is weird. Should we go up?"

"Why not? We've come this far. Let's keep going and see what happens." They crept up the next flight of stairs and into their familiar hallway. The door was partway open. Fearing the worst, David peered around the door at Miss Hansen. She faced the board, leading the class in a Language Arts lesson.

"She doesn't see us," he whispered to Julia. She shook her head. "…but what about the kids? They'll probably laugh or call out to us when we go in."

"I know, but we've gotta get back inside. Here goes."

Julia took off into the room. David closed his eyes for a moment, took a deep breath and then followed.

No one seemed to notice as they tip-toed back to their seats. Just then, the bell rang for dismissal. Books were slammed shut as Miss Hansen called out the homework assignment. Nobody listened.

David and Julia joined the rest of their classmates who scrambled towards the door. David's friend Rolley met David there, and they squeezed through the doorframe together. David tried to get away from Rolley, but Rolley matched strides with him. "What are you gonna do today after school?"

"Uh-er, I don't know," mumbled David, sure Rolley would ask him why he had climbed out the window and later returned through the door.

Rolley didn't seem to have anything on his mind but a video game. "Did you know I got to level 30 yesterday? Better than Damien and Buzz. Damien has 18 and Buzz has 10. Ha!"

As Rolley rambled on, David looked for Julia. She was descending the stairs, surrounded by several girls. The others were talking excitedly about something, but Julia looked reflective. She was smiling kind of smugly and dreamily. Her eyes met David's. She gave him a questioning look. He shrugged and looked down.

Did it really happen? Did we leave the school with the dove, see a whirlwind, a treasure chest and go into a cave? Did we see a wonderful fire? What did it all mean? Those questions spun around in David's head for the next three days and nights, keeping him distracted by day and sleepless at night.

CHAPTER FIVE
MEETING THE DAY

The fourth morning after the adventures rose bright and clear. As David awakened, his thoughts bounced around. He remembered the dove, the tree and the tent. Why had he seen those things? Maybe it was all just a dream.

But no, Julia saw that dove too. Not only the dove but all those other things: the whirlwind, the treasure chest and the fire in the cave. They both saw them. But why? Maybe he was chosen because he was that knight in the dreams, brave, honest and worthy of honor.

David stumbled to the mirror. He was disappointed at what he saw. He squinted and peered closer-without his glasses he could barely see.

Naw, that couldn't be. Look at me. I'm a nerd. I love to study and read about medieval kingdoms instead of playing sports like the other kids. I'm no knight. Nobody wants to hang out with me.

David did have one, maybe two friends, Rolley and Julia. Julia didn't have many friends at school yet. She was courageous, but not in the heroine kind-of-way. Gazing at his morning flyaway hair, he groaned. His jet-black hair always stood out in a sea of blonds and redheads. What a loser.

His family didn't fit in, either. His father was a carpenter and an unsuccessful farmer, not like the other parents who were doctors and lawyers. His mother always embarrassed him in public with her "different" ways. Once, she even rode a donkey into town to get him to the Emergency Room when the car was out of gas. The other kids laughed about it for weeks.

David went to his bureau and pulled out his shirt and underwear. Then he walked sleepily to the closet and grabbed the hanger with his school uniform. Wrinkled, but it would do. He finished dressing, put on his glasses and stared straight ahead. Thoughts came quickly to him now.

And now this happens. The bird, Evod. Why did it choose me, David Roth? And why Julia?

As he thought about Julia and himself, the morning bell rang, and he turned to face his fellow fifth graders. He walked down the hall with his head down, barely noticing the other kids and ignoring their comments.

"Hey, watch where you're going!"

"He better not try to sit with us!"

"Wake up, sleepy-head!"

David ate his breakfast alone. He had a sinking feeling in his stomach that no amount of cereal could fill. He wanted desperately to fit in with the other kids, but how could that ever happen? This was too much to bear!

CHAPTER SIX
JULIA IN THE MORNING

That same morning, Julia woke up feeling afraid. She couldn't stop thinking about what she had seen; the dove, the tree, the meadow and the cave. It all seemed so fun and exciting at the time, but now it was overwhelming her!

Why would this all happen to me? I'm the new kid at school. Nobody even knows me here. That thought made her uneasy.

Things were different today. She had Secrets. She was sure it would be all over her face when the other students saw her. The whole school would be looking. What would she say if they started asking questions?

Julia pulled the covers over her head and tried to breathe. Even though the musty wool of the blanket choked off most of her oxygen, at least she was safe there.

Nobody will believe me if I tell them what I saw! And this David kid...does he know what's going on? He said he doesn't. He seems nice enough- but is he going to tell and get me in trouble? ..... Again? Like at the other schools?

"Oh, Oh." Julia sobbed as these fears came crashing down on her the fourth time since she had gone to bed-it had been so difficult to sleep in her dorm room. She had awakened four times in a panic but managed to go back to sleep three of those times. Thankfully, her roommates were early risers and had left hours before.

Two girls came jogging into the room. One was Julia's roommate, Amanda. The other was Amanda's friend, Tori. They had just returned from an early morning jog with the Running Club.

"What's the matter?" they asked, almost simultaneously.

"Nothing," squeaked Julia from beneath the sheets and blankets. "Just a bad dream."

"Oh," said Tori. "Want to talk about it?"

Julia could tell by the tone of her voice that Tori really didn't want to talk about it. *She probably just wants to get to her room and get dressed for the day. That's good, because I don't want to talk about it at all. It will be hard enough to get out of bed and face everyone and pretend nothing happened. But maybe that's it, nothing happened!*

Right then and there, Julia decided to tell herself that nothing had happened. Over and over, she repeated the denials to herself. She felt both courage and calmness rise in her, and she sat up and said evenly, "No, I'm fine."

CHAPTER SEVEN
NAPLES CHRISTIAN ACADEMY

"David! I'm so glad you're home." Mom squeezed her arms around him. "How was your week at school?"

David wriggled out of his mother's arms and frowned. "Oh, Mom, nobody likes me there. Some kids get all the attention, and some, like me, get none."

"I'm so sorry to hear that, David. It's not supposed to be like that."

He certainly felt special at home. At bedtime, Mom often would sing softly and tell stories about a kingdom that his family knew about. "There was always a wonderful feeling there, the people's language was love, and everything was peaceful and kind. In this far off place, every person was a relative - a "brother" or a "sister." All were related and equally important. No one was treated better than another."

"This seems like a fairy-tale place. How can it be?"

"Well," she had replied. "The king makes sure of it. He rules with love and requires all the people there to walk in love too."

David enjoyed thinking about such a king. When he was little, David made up his name, The King of the Star, because of the golden star on Mom's necklace he focused on when she talked.

Sometimes, in his dreams, he visited the kingdom. David was always a brave knight in the kingdom and rode a steely-hard, magnificent, black horse. He had a large star on his shield and breastplate and fought against the awful armies of the evil King of the Moon. The people of that kingdom spoke the language of hate, fear and jealousy. Most nights, he won the battle for his King of the Star, to whom he was dedicated as a loyal soldier.

CHAPTER EIGHT
FINDING THE STAR

"Come on, David." Julia had approached David's desk in the empty classroom after school. "Let's go to the basement and see what's going on down there."

"Who me? No, I'm not going down there. There's nothing to see."

"How can you be so sure? Let's go. We've got to find out what this is all about."

"No, I'm sure it's nothing. Leave me alone."

"Okay, your choice."

As Julia turned to leave, a tug inside David made him want to follow her. "Ok. wait…" he called out, "I'll go crazy if I don't look down there. I'm coming, but we won't find anything." He followed her down the two flights of stairs. As they opened the door, they saw no fire, no mysterious fog. Just the normal basement, which was the old sanctuary of a church. Now it was filled with bookshelves and file cabinets and was used for storage.

"I told you there was nothing." David was relieved at first, but then disappointed there was no Evod or fire down there.

"Aw, shucks, you were right." Julia said. "But maybe there's something else mysterious we can find."

"Well, maybe there's a book here that can explain about the fire…eh…what we saw down here," he suggested. David liked to find answers to his questions in books. As he started to make his way through the clutter to a dust-covered bookshelf, a loud whooshing noise filled the basement. The dove! David almost fell over with surprise as he arched his back and followed Evod with his eyes. "Now I'm sure there must be something here!"

The dove settled on an old safe. Both kids eagerly waded through the dusty debris. As they got closer to the safe, Evod launched upward and hovered in the upper corner of the room, watching.

The children dug around until they could get the safe opened easily.

"Something's inside." David called out excitedly as he stuck his hand towards the bottom of the drawer. He pulled out an object wrapped in a shiny white cloth. Strange writing was written all over it. Julia eagerly grabbed it too and they started to remove the outer layer together. Underneath, they found another layer, this one of white paper. As they unwrapped this layer, the paper became hot in their hands.

"It's hot!" Julia let go of it and held her breath as David continued unwrapping. "Ouch! That hurts!" He pulled his hands back quickly and dropped the object to the floor. They crouched in front of it. David reached out and tried again. This time, the paper came off easily. Inside was a glass star. It was blue and white and had six points. Twelve outer triangles alternated blue and white, starting at the top. This ring of triangles was secured by straight lines of silver which formed a pattern. The center of the glass star was cut out and outlined in silver.

"The star! I know this star!" cried David. His mind flashed to visions of the stars in his home and of the king in his dreams.

"I've never seen a star like that," Julia said.

The dove circled the children and disappeared through a closed window.

"Did you see that?" Julia exclaimed.

"I sure did! How did it get out?" David quickly handed the star to Julia and pushed his way to the window. He peered through the smudged panes, then turned and looked at Julia.

"The dove led us here. We're supposed to have-" He pointed to the star.

"That!" Now he was determined to continue following Evod.

Julia looked skeptically at David, then the star. "Well, I guess nobody will miss it." She shrugged.

David walked back to Julia, and carefully took the star from her. He felt instant peace. He had the deeper feeling that the star was worth far more than the jewels they had seen in the field. Without taking his eyes off the star, he said, "I'd better take it and show it to my parents. They may know more about it, and where it came from."

"Do you think so David?"

"I know so. I'm going home this weekend. I'll just keep it 'til then." He looked towards the window again. "Evod was here …It must be important."

Footsteps crossed overhead, and both kids jumped. "We better be quiet. If they find us here, detention for sure," David whispered as he quickly re-wrapped the star and slid it into his backpack.

CHAPTER NINE
CONFIDING IN DAVID'S PARENTS

"Mom, Dad, I have something to show you." David opened his backpack in his family's foyer and produced the star. He gently laid it on the small table the Roths used to collect keys and other valuables.

"Aah," gasped his mother from behind him. "The star!"

"Where did you get this, son?" asked his dad, coming in from the driveway. "Well, I found it in the basement of the school – the old sanctuary."

"And what were you doing down there?" Dad put his hands on his hips and glared at David.

David sheepishly looked down. "Snooping around."

"David ---"

"Oh Jacob, what does that matter? David found the star! THE star. The one our whole family and faith and even the school is built upon! Leave him alone!"

"Mom, what are you saying?" Mom got on her knees in front of him and began weeping. "I'm saying you found something that has been missing for a long, long time, Honey." She wiped her eyes.

"Your great-grandfather Moishe brought that star over from Europe and used it to start the school. And it's a miracle you have found it - a real miracle."

The family's radio had been playing quietly in the background. A song that said someone's been walking with you for a long time came on the radio. David stopped and listened. Those words seemed powerful to him at that moment.

Dad let out a low whistle and shook his head a few times. "That's pretty amazing! We didn't think it would ever be found again."

"It was lost? No way. It was right there in the basement." David couldn't believe it.

"How did you know where to look?" Mom asked.

"Well..." He thought of Julia, and the dove and everything that had happened. *TMI for now*, he told himself. "I didn't know to look for it. I just found it."

Dad said, "Well, there's only one thing to be done. You give it to Mr. Aark, on Monday morning."

"Are you sure Dad?" David wasn't sure giving the star to the principal was a good idea.

"David, this star needs to go back to the school."

"But doesn't it belong to us? Our family? It's like Mom's star. The school didn't take good care of it." David felt like he was pleading to keep the star. It surprised him. "It's important that Mr. Aark has it and displays it for all the students to see. It's what Mom's grandfather wanted." His mother looked deep into his eyes and nodded.

"Why?" David stood up and faced his father in

defiance.

His mom's voice broke in. "Because Grandpa Moishe used the star to start the school. It was real important to him at the time…and important to the school. And the other children need to know about the star too. Its history is, well, why they are all there."

David palmed his forehead. "I'm confused."

His mother said, "I know, Son, it has been confusing for a long time, but you finding the star will start to bring clarity."

More mysteries. David couldn't wait to tell Julia on Monday. He repacked the star into his backpack.

David's father interrupted his thoughts, "David, do you want me to go with you to deliver the star?"

"No, Dad I can do it myself." With Julia.

CHAPTER TEN
MEL

On the way to class Monday morning, David ran into Mel, the janitor. Mel had been the farmhand for David's family for many years. People called him the "Master Gardener" because he knew so much about trees, plants, and well, lots of things. David's parents respected his wisdom a lot, and they had often asked his opinion about the types of trees to plant, how to fix a washing machine, and even questions about God and the afterlife. David respected him too, having followed him around the farm as a toddler, and forming a strong bond with Mel.

David called out "I'm so happy to see you!" David reminded himself of the times Mel's face at school helped reduce the home sickness he felt for the farm, his parents and baby brother, Albert.

David walked into the janitor's closet and proudly opened his backpack to show Mel what he and Julia had found. Mel looked at the star and smiled broadly. "So, you found it, David. You found the star."

"Yes, Mel, what does it mean?"

"What does it mean? Well, it's your destiny, er, all our destinies. It's an amazing ancient symbol. It can unlock deep mysteries and teach us about ourselves, our purposes, and even how to get along with each other."

David was puzzled as he stared up at Mel. Mel continued, "You must have heard about the Bethlehem or Christmas star?"

David brightened, "Sure, Mel. I was even born under the Christmas star, on Christmas Day at the Star of Bethlehem Hospital. At least that's what I've been told my whole life." They both chuckled.

"Most people have heard about that star," Mel continued. "Well, here is this other star." He was silent for a moment as he smiled at the star. Then he said, "Hardly anyone puts the two stars together. But He does."

"He?"

Mel, looked up. "The dove."

"The dove, what dove?" David pretended not to know what Mel was talking about.

"The dove that's been following you around and taking you on adventures."

David couldn't hold back any longer. "Uh…How did you know that? Who told you?"

Just then, Julia appeared in the doorway.

"Mel, tell Julia what you just told me!"

"Well, just that the star is connected to the dove that keeps following David and you around."

David blurted out, "I knew it! I knew it… the dove and the star,"

Julia looked at Mel and stammered, "You know about the dove?"

Mel responded, "Yes, of course, I've known about him all my life."

David couldn't contain his excitement. "Tell us what you know…"

Julia chimed in, "Yes, tell us."

Mel spoke slowly and began to pace a few steps each direction as he said, "Well, basically, the dove came first, then after a while, the star. Your family, David, are descendants of the Children of the Star. They kept these secrets. Then other families, like yours, Julia," He stopped in front of her and smiled- "started following the dove. They are the Children of the Cross. The problem is—" Mel crossed his arms and leaned against his desk- "a canyon developed between the Children of the Cross and the Children of the Star. Because of that canyon of misunderstanding, a lot of great things that were supposed to be for both people were lost."

"Like the star?" David moved closer to Mel.

"Yes, David, like the star." Mel rubbed his grey-bearded chin and looked deep in thought. "You see, kids, the star is a symbol of what was lost. It was lost to the school for a long time and now that the dove has led you to it, well, lots of things will start opening up to you- mysteries that have been forgotten."

Julia stood there, wide-eyed. Finally, she spoke. "Wow, I never heard that before."

"My mom said something like that this weekend," David said.

All three of them were silent for a while. Then Mel ducked out of the closet and into his larger office. He returned with a thick book.

34

"Now that you've seen the dove, and He led you to the star, you should have this book. Your great-grandfather wrote it, David" He held out the book. "It should connect the

Children of the Star to the Children of the Cross. Read this and you'll learn a lot more."

David took the old leather-covered book. It felt heavy in his hands.

"Read this? And then... what? What do we do about all this other stuff?"

"Well, David. First you decide if it's important to you. Then find out everything you can. Find out why the dove came to school. Why he led you to the star. This quest will be life changing."

David barely managed to speak, "Life changing?" His eyes grew big.

Mel nodded, "Then share it with others. It's important not just for you two, but for the school and your families and even beyond that." Mel closed some open cabinets and drawers. Then he turned back to the children with a big smile. "Please know I'm always willing to talk about it. In fact, I want to hear about everything you learn. I really respect the star. Make sure you always treat it and these other things with respect."

They nodded silently. It was a lot to take in, but they wanted to understand. They would read this book. And they would keep the star, at least for a while. David gently rewrapped the star and eased it into his backpack. "Ok, Mel, we will do what you say."

CHAPTER ELEVEN
OPENING THE BOOK

"David, I had a crazy dream last night!" Julia whispered to David as he found his seat in class the next morning. Julia pretended to copy down the spelling words Miss Hansen wrote on the board. "It was about the Kingdom of the Star."

"It was? I had a dream about the Kingdom too." David whispered back. "I had the star on my shield as I rode on a white horse!" He tossed his pencil on the floor in front of Julia to get closer to her.

"I was on a horse too, but I had a cross on my shield." She kept her eyes lowered and doodled in her notebook.

David remained crouched on the floor. "It was some battle! But I don't know who we were fighting."

"Me neither. Who could it be David? There were black horses, but I didn't see any faces."

"No way- same dream!"

"David, better read that book Mel gave you. Something is going on." "I agree Julia- afterschool?" David barely got the words out of his mouth when

Miss Hansen walked towards their end of the classroom and stared at them. He scrambled to his desk. It seemed like forever for school to end that day. David and Julia each grabbed an armful of books and waited on the bench outside the classroom door until everyone, including Miss Hansen, left the building.

Then, David and Julia took his great-grandfather's book and hurried down to the basement.

"Open it, David!"

"Introduction. This book is the personal account of Moses Solomon Blum. It tells of my life, my faith and the beginning of Naples Christian Academy.

I started the school in September of 1954. I was the first principal, and now my son, Aaron Matthew Blum is its principal. The school was founded upon the connection between the Jewish roots and grafted- in Gentile branches of the olive tree spoken of in Romans 11:17 of the Bible.

I wanted to make sure that the full picture of the Christian faith was embraced.

I created several Stars of David in glass and silver when I lived in Naples, Italy. Some were sold, but one particular star came with me to America and inspired the founding of Naples Christian Academy in Belbridge, New Hampshire."

"Wow, my grandpa's father really did start the school! And HE made the star!" David's eyes grew big.

David turned to the Table of Contents. "Fire Worship...Let's give this a try." He flipped the pages.

"Chapter Five, Fire Worship. 'Fire can be a the-the- theophany, a physical sign that reveals God is present.'"

"Hmmm." David slowly thumbed some more pages and read, 'There are parallels between God and Fire ... throughout the book of Exodus in the Old Testament we see fire. Some examples are the burning bush Moses saw, and the fire by night and the pillar of cloud that appeared before the Israelites coming out of Egypt.'"

He stopped. "I think I know about the burning bush. Isn't that where Moses was told to take off his shoes?"

David looked down into the heavy book. "Oh yeah, here it is! Exodus 3:1-5. "Then the angel of Adonai appeared to him in a flame of fire from within a bush. So, he looked and saw the bush burning with fire, yet it was not consumed.'" David looked at Julia. "Those words are right from the Bible," he told her. "Then it says further down, Adonai said 'Come no closer. Take your sandals off your feet, for the place where you are standing is holy ground.'" (Holy Bible. Tree of Life Version, Baker Books, The Messianic Jewish Family Bible Society, 2015.)

Julia called out, "Well if that's true, we blew it...we didn't take off our shoes or anything!"

"I know."

"And we didn't see a burning bush! We just saw a fire." Julia sounded disappointed. "That doesn't explain what we saw."

"I know, Julia," David replied, "But we did see fire, and that can be a theophany. This basement was an old church, so now it's starting to make sense that a fire would be here. It says here the fire by night was a huge fire that led the people. I know the dove led us to the fire and the star. But why?" David flipped through the front of the book. "Here's another chapter: 'The Eternal Flame in Judaism and Christian belief systems.'" He cleared his throat and read, 'God told Moses that a lamp filled with pure oil should always burn in the Tabernacle. Jewish synagogues today follow this instruction. Christian churches burn a similar lamp continually as well, to show that the light of Christ always burns in a sin-darkened world.'"

Julia sighed. "Well, the fire's out now."

"Yes, the fire is out…. Seriously!" He smiled. "But I'm gonna take this book and read it some more."

As they walked back to their dorms in the fading sunlight, David turned to Julia. "I don't get all of this stuff, but it sounds familiar."

Julia nodded her head. "I remember Moses from Sunday School- I went a few times when I was younger. They told us about him."

David was surprised. "Wait. But I thought Moses was … for OUR people- the Jewish people!"

"Oh, no, WE have him, too."

"You can't. Moses belongs to us."

"I'm telling you, David. I learned about Moses."

"How could you-" David's face turned red and he grabbed Julia's backpack to pull it off her shoulder. He'd show her.

Julia made a fist and raised it towards David's arm.

They stopped and glared angrily at each other. David couldn't believe Julia thought she knew about Moses. Why, didn't she just hear the name Moses was in his family- his great grandfather who wrote the book - the one they called Moishe, had been named after the famous Moses. "We can't both have him."

"Why not?"

After a moment, they both burst into laughter.

"This is silly." Julia giggled.

"Yeah," said David. "Why fight about a guy that isn't even alive anymore?"

Julia sighed. "We can both have him."

"Sounds good to me." David grinned. "I guess the Children of the Star and the Children of the Cross could be on the same team."

CHAPTER TWELVE
SECRETS

"We will have to keep this stuff to ourselves."
David leaned over Julia at lunch and whispered,
"And I'm still not giving the star to Mr. Aark!"

Julia looked up from her phone and squinted into
the sun. "Why not?"

"The less people that know, the less we can get
into trouble….at least until we find out what's going
on."

Julia agreed and over the next few days, they
spoke together in hushed tones at breakfast, lunch
and recess.

Towards the end of class the following week,
while the others were busy putting their books away,
David approached Julia's desk. "There's danger
someone might hear us. Let's walk out of the
building separately and meet behind the bleachers at
the soccer field."

"Okay, good idea."

David left the classroom first and paced behind
the bleachers. Julia met up with him a few minutes
later. Julia looked around for eavesdroppers, then
said, "I feel this tingling in my chest when we talk

about this stuff."

David touched his chest. "Me too. I guess it's the excitement of keeping secrets."

"Hey David, did you see Rolley staring at us during Math today?"

"Yeah, I felt his eyes on me." David chuckled. "I decided to stare him down, but when I looked at him, he made a face and stuck his tongue out."

Julia's mouth flew open. "He didn't!"

David wrinkled his nose. "I guess he's really mad at me for talking to you so much."

Julia nodded. "Don't feel bad, David. Amanda sidled up to me in the dorm last night and asked me what was going on with you and me. I told her nothing. She said she saw us off by ourselves at recess." Julia flicked a piece of bread off her shoe. "I had to think quick, so I said we were doing a project for Miss Hansen. I don't think she believed me." Julia looked at David.

David frowned, then quickly scanned the lawn. "Great, now she'll probably be watching us all the time."

By the end of the week, the whole school had decided that David and Julia were "weird". Maybe, some said, they were playing Dungeons and Dragons or some other fantasy game. Others thought they might be boyfriend and girlfriend. Eeeewww!

Friday afternoon, Rolley asked David, "Hey, dude, are you and Julia playing some sort of fantasy game at recess? We've noticed you sneaking off and talking together."

David gulped hard. His mind searched frantically for an answer. "Um, yeah. That's it…a fantasy game…It's called…Uh…AS YOU WISH."

"As You Wish?" Rolley snorted, "What kind of game is that?"

"Well, you have to think of a weird adventure and the other person asks questions about it."

"Oh, okay, I see. Can I try it sometime?"

"Uh, sure. But you might think it's boring."

"Yeah, you're right, David, I might." Rolley was already looking over at the kickball game on the other side of the playground.

David didn't feel too bad about lying since his description was actually very close to the truth. The conversations he had with Julia really were about the "weird" adventures they'd had and trying to guess what would happen next. So, from then on, David and Julia had a cover story for their withdrawals and whispering. And it wasn't lying, exactly.

CHAPTER THIRTEEN
TAKING THE STAR TO MR. AARK

During his regular Wednesday night phone call with his mother, David was put on the spot again.

"David, Dad wants to know if you gave the star to Mr. Aark yet."

"Uh, no Mom," David stammered. "It's just that I've been so busy with my book project, I haven't had time to go to the office." David sat on his bed and shook his ankle. He cleared his throat. "Anyway, I heard that Mr. Aark has been out of town for a few days."

"Well, okay, David," his mother said. "But you know your father and I want you to give it to him." She sighed. "Do you think you can do it tomorrow?"

David tried to think of something to say. He didn't want to lie or hide things from Mom, but he knew he wasn't in any hurry to turn the star in."

"Okay, Mom. I'll see if I can." David looked around his dorm room for an excuse to get off the phone. For once, he wished his roommates were there to interrupt him. "Uh, I'd better go now. Gotta get ready for bed."

"Okay, dear. Sweet dreams. I love you. Talk to

you soon."

"Love you too, Mom." Guilt swept over him. How long could he keep lying to his mom?

A few days later, David saw Julia walking down the hallway during Free Time after lunch.

"Did you find out anything new?" Julia asked.

David shook his head.

"Well, I've been thinking." Julia walked closer. "We really better take the star and show it to Mr. Aark."

"Are you crazy?" David threw his hands in the air but quickly pulled them back down when another student walked by. "We decided this must be OUR secret!"

"But how can keeping it a secret help anyone?" Julia stomped her foot.

"Help anyone? Who says that it's supposed to help anyone?" David whispered loudly.

"Your parents. Mel. Oh, David, come on. Do you think Evod showed it to us just so only we could know about it?" Julia motioned to a bench near where they were standing outside the gym.

David sat down. He looked at the tiled floor.

"Well…I s-s-suppose …" stuttered David. "But I think we might get in trouble for snooping around in the basement." David recognized that old friend, FEAR. He sat up straight and shivered slightly.

"We should take it to Mr. Aark." Julia folded her arms across her chest. "As soon as possible."

"Are you sure?" David shifted his weight from his right to left thigh. "I'm not so sure he's a fan of the Star. Can we trust him?"

Julia sighed. "I don't know, but your parents said

it's something the school lost. We don't want to be accused of stealing. We don't know what to do with it. Maybe Mr. Aark will."

He grinned and nodded at Julia. "Ok, Let's hope we're doing the right thing." Julia led David down the hallway and across the wide lobby area to the Administration Office. There was a reception desk outside the principal's door.

"Um, we need to see Mr. Aark please," Julia said politely as she moved up to the desk and rested her fingertips on its glass top.

The nosey secretary looked Julia up and down. "I'm sorry, young lady. You need an appointment. Come back tomorrow after school. Mr. Aark should be free then." She started to turn away.

"Tomorrow?" Julia said. "We can't wait until then." David peeked his head around Julia's shoulders and lifted the star for Mrs. Barrey to see. A look of shock spread across her face.

"Uh, er… I'll see what I can do." She jabbed the intercom button that rang in Mr. Aark's office. "Mr. Aark, I have an urgent matter here. I need to interrupt you," she whispered hoarsely. Her eyes darted back and forth between the children and the hallway behind them.

Mr. Aark emerged from his office with disheveled hair and a sleepy look on his face. "Yes, Mrs. Barrey, what is it?" He looked up and caught David's eye and saw the star. He staggered backwards.

"Mr. Roth," he said gruffly, "Follow me."

David led the way confidently now, as a confused Julia followed. They entered the principal's office. Mr. Aark's body language changed. David thought he seemed nervous. He sat down at his desk and raised two steely blue eyes to the children, who were now at eye level.

"Now tell me why you are here." His eyes went to the star and stayed there.

Julia moved forward and blurted, "Well, Mr. Aark, we found this star, and well, we think it might be important."

"Important? No, I don't think so." He shook his head and looked down for a moment. Abruptly, he looked up at them again. "Where did you find it?" His eyes pierced right through them.

This time David spoke. "In the basement, Mr. Aark, and we think it might have something to do with this school and my great-grandfather."

"You were in the basement?" he shouted angrily. "You know the basement is off limits! I am extremely disappointed in you two. You are two of my best students! That is one week after school detention." Mr. Aark grabbed his detention pad and started writing furiously.

"We're sorry, Mr. Aark." David looked at Julia. "We won't do it again," he managed to say, before his throat closed.

"No, we won't do it again. But what about the star? And the school?" Julia said, as she spread her arms.

"Pooh, pooh, I'm sure it's not important…" Mr. Aark shook his head, then stopped and looked at the children. "but what about the school?"

"Well, David's parents said it's something the school lost, and we just wanted to bring it back to you."

"What? To me? Why would I want it?" Mr. Aark spat out the words.

David and Julia looked at each other. They didn't know what to say.

"Humph." Mr. Aark stood up. "Well, I'll look into it." He grabbed the star

from David and put it into an empty cabinet. "In the meantime, I'll keep it

in here for safe keeping." He opened the office door for them and they hurried out.

David turned to Julia as they walked, and said, "Satisfied? Do you think he will take care of the star?"

"I – I guess so," Julia said slowly, "but I'm disappointed about our detentions."

"Me, too." David's face turned red. "I told you we'd get in trouble!"

"I'm really mad too. I can't believe that man." Julia raised two clenched fists. "Mr. Aark doesn't think we're important. He doesn't have time for us, just like my father."

David scowled. "I hate to say it, but I told you so."

CHAPTER FOURTEEN
DAVID AND THE BULLIES

A few days after the visit to Mr. Aark's office, the boys from David's class were out on the soccer field for PE. Scotty and Keith and some of the other boys were playing soccer. As David walked near one of the goalposts, Bam! Everything went dark. Pain exploded in his brain. Gradually he opened his eyes. *What happened?*

The boys laughed. "Good shot, Scotty," he heard someone say. One of the boys had hit David in the forehead with the soccer ball!

David hung on to the ball for support and tried to stand up. From somewhere, he heard, "Hey, give us the ball!"

He was still wobbling on his feet when Scotty repeated angrily, "Hey nerd, give us our ball. We've got to practice for the game today."

"Ball…game?" David's mind was still fuzzy.

"Give it back."

"Hey, cut it out, Scotty, can't you see he's hurt?" Rolley yelled.

"Hurt, shmurt. He's a skinny little baby, no wonder he couldn't make the team."

Keith ran up to David. "Hey, you give us that ball, or we will tell Coach Buford!" Keith turned and let out a yell in the opposite direction, "Hey Coach, David took our ball!" A grey-haired man in a jogging suit came running over.

"What seems to be the problem, boys?" He spread his legs apart, crossed his arms and smiled at Scotty and Keith. "These two are keeping us from practicing!" Keith sneered.

"Yeah," chimed in Scotty.

"What's your name again, young man?" David's own PE teacher didn't seem to know who he was. The coach frowned at David and Rolley.

"David Roth."

"Well, David, give the ball back and march yourself right into Mr. Aark's office. I'll deal with you later." He nodded toward the school.

Hurting and confused, David walked slowly to the school building. When he looked back, he saw Coach Buford and the boys on the soccer team laughing hysterically. He didn't see Rolley.

When David shuffled into the Administration area, Mr. Aark did not seem surprised to see him. "Take a seat, young man. What seems to be the problem, this time?" David sat down on the green leather chair next to Mrs. Barrey's desk. Pointing outside, David said, "Coach Buford sent me in. He said to wait."

Coach Buford showed up fifteen minutes later, but it seemed like an hour to David. The Coach didn't look at David. "Mr. Aark, we seem to have a problem with attitude from Mr. Roth. He blocked the boys' soccer practice today, and he hasn't been doing the assigned exercises in PE."

"Really?" Mr. Aark's eyebrows and the corner of his lip went up. He sat on the arm of a chair next to David and leaned forward. "We'll have to see about this. David, why did you block the game?"

"I didn't. They hit me--"

Before David could finish, Mr. Aark blurted out, "I've had enough of your insubordination. First the basement, now this. In addition to the after-school detention you and Julia are doing, you will serve …. Let's see…. what would be appropriate?" Mr. Aark tapped his chin a few times. "Oh yes. You will have to do some work around the school. You can… help the janitor. Yes, you can help Mel clean the bathrooms and do all his other," he coughed, "chores. Every day after your detention. I hope that will teach you a lesson, Mr. Roth."

The principal disappeared into his office. Coach Buford put his hand over his mouth, but David could see he was grinning as he rushed back to the field. David examined his hands and wondered what had just happened. He couldn't think of anything he had done wrong on the soccer field.

Mr. Aark returned with a slip of paper. He shoved it at David. "Here, take this to the Janitor's closet. Mel will know what to do."

David stood up and slowly moved his head from side to side to clear his vision. He took the slip and went off to look for Mel. David was furious that the players, coach and now even the principal had not come to his aid after he was hit. He was relieved when he saw Mel and told him what had happened.

Mel looked surprised but smiled and told him "It's all for the best, David. You'll see."

David soon found that working with Mel was lots of fun. They chatted as he and Mel swept and waxed the floors and Mel fixed a couple of the sinks around the school. After a few days, David realized it was a perfect opportunity to ask Mel about the book and Evod. He got up his courage and asked, "Mel, why didn't anyone at the school or in the church tell me about the star?"

Mel didn't seem surprised by the question. In fact, it seemed like he was waiting for it. "I'm glad you asked, David." He sat down on a small stool. "There were, and still are, some people that don't want you or anyone else to know," Mel said. "Unfortunately, that's the way more division, misunderstanding and hatred can flourish. But hatred is not the way of the Kingdom of the Star." He shook his head.

"So, there **is** a Kingdom of the Star?" David felt a jolt run through his body. He crouched next to Mel.

"There sure is," replied Mel.

"Is it a real kingdom?" David put down his tools. "How do we get there? I see it in my dreams."

"You do? That's good." Mel smiled warmly at David. His eyes twinkled. "Oh, it's very real. Evod is leading you there." Mel moved his hand through the air. "He is giving you access to it through the adventures you've experienced."

"Why doesn't he just come out and show us the whole kingdom?"

"Then it wouldn't be something you discovered.

You would take it for granted." Mel stood up and handed David a wet mop.

David looked up at the ceiling. "For granted?" He began to mop and tried to figure out what Mel meant.

Mel chuckled. "This way it's like a treasure hunt. It's more satisfying when you find the treasure, and what you learn along the way stays with you forever." He turned and picked up another mop.

David stopped and looked straight ahead. "The treasure chest was weird. Julia and I thought we wanted it, but in the end we didn't."

"You chose the way less traveled, that is, the way most kids wouldn't have chosen." Mel patted David on the back and grinned. "And that brought you to the cave—deeper things. It was a kind of test."

"And we passed, Mel?"

"You both passed, David." They finished the day with contented smiles on their faces.

News of David's after school job got around fast. Later that week, Scotty and Keith were waiting for David as he walked upstairs to his classroom. At the doorway, Scotty whispered, "Janitor Boy." Stunned, David tripped across the threshold towards his seat.

"Junior Janitor," Keith yelled out. The whole class, except for Julia and Rolley, burst into laughter.

David's face became hot. He tried to look busy and focused on opening his binder, but he felt everyone's eyes on him.

"Hey, how do you like being the maid's little helper?" asked another boy from the soccer team. Miss Hansen called the class to order with a clap and glared at all the boys at the same time.

David's heart eventually slowed down, and he began listening to the teacher. The minutes ticked by and it was time for lunch.

In the cafeteria, David's regular table was empty. There usually were lots of boys there. Scotty walked by. "Nobody wants to smell the garbage and cleaning spray on your hands, David!" The lunchroom erupted into howls of laughter.

David looked down and began to eat slowly. After a few bites he looked up. Julia and Rolley had slipped onto the bench beside him. *At least they are standing by me.*

CHAPTER FIFTEEN
GOING TO BIG CHAPEL

Two weeks later, David felt the excitement in the air as if it were a balloon filled with helium. He hurried as he dressed for weekly chapel.

Rolley, who had proved to be a good friend, was David's roommate. He said, "I can't believe we'll finally get to sit with the grownups today. We won't have to be with the little kids anymore."

"...and listen to those babyish stories." David added.

Buzz, his other roommate walked up to the mirror and grimaced. "Do we really have to wear these Jackets?"

"You know we do. Remember, Dorm Master Robbins told us the rule for this chapel: all boys wear navy blazers." David said as he straightened his tie.

"What about the girls? Do they have to dress up?" Rolley squeaked.

"Sure do. They have to wear – dresses!" David smiled, thinking of how much Julia hated dresses.

Laughter. "I feel sorry for them!" said Buzz.

Sharply at 8:10, Dorm Master Robbins, the Head of the Boys' Dormitory, knocked on the door. The boys snapped to attention. "Time for breakfast," the headmaster shouted through the thick oak door. "Be ready in five minutes!" Then they heard Mr. Robbins walking away.

The boys giggled and took turns lightly punching each other in the stomach. David was nervous but he was glad to have these guys to joke around with him. They finished dressing, and stood awkwardly in a sort of line, staring at the door.

Precisely five minutes later, the door flew open. Headmaster Robbins' head appeared, slanted to the side as he stared down at his ten-year-old charges. The usual bored look on Mr. Robbins' face was replaced with a look of surprise, even shock.

"You are ready? ALL ready? Altogether ready?" (Dorm Master Robbins was British)

"Yes, Sir." David replied.

"Very well, then," said Headmaster Robbins, blinking his eyes rapidly. "Follow me."

David and the other boys had taken these steps hundreds of times. David could have walked into the breakfast room blindfolded; however, this day was different from all other days. The excitement of going to "Big Chapel" cast a hazy glow over everything. David nudged Buzz who was in front of him. "Hey, do you think these stairs look different today?"

Buzz reared back and made a face, "Nah, you're crazy. I don't know what you're talking about."

Rolley sprinted forward and appeared at David's left elbow. "Yeah, David, I think you're right. Things seem kind of blurry today."

In the large breakfast room, everyone took their

places quickly. The servers at each table were ready to pour water, orange juice and milk. They began without any commotion. These junior high kids were serious about their work, as they had earned their positions by proving to be reliable and detail-oriented.

David couldn't eat. The butterflies in his stomach had nothing to do with Rolley's fake punch earlier. What would they see in the big church?

He found Julia in the crowded room. Pulling her aside, he whispered, "What do you think could be going on with the adults? Have they seen what we've seen?"

"I was thinking the same thing," said Julia. "Have they seen Evod too? Do they know about the star?"

"I don't know if that would be good or bad." said David.

Julia shook her head. "Me neither."

"Nice dress," David said, smiling.

"Yeah, thanks." Julia looked down and frowned at her outfit. Then she looked at David again. "But I can tell you, I can't wait either. My whole body is vibrating with excitement and a new kind of strange fear." She shivered all over.

David put his hand on his stomach. "I couldn't eat the buttered toast, scrambled eggs and orange slices like I usually do. "Today, my stomach is rattling and pulsing, threatening to erupt from either direction."

They both laughed.

The bell rang for the children's church. The younger boys and girls scampered out, like they always did, laughing and chattering, and poking each other in the ribs as they wound their way down the stairs into the classrooms.

Funny, David felt so much older now. Then he remembered what he had found in the basement. The fire and the star! David's heart pumped a few extra beats on top of the already fast pace it was beating. He closed his eyes and prayed that no one else would see anything down there. The secrets were between him and Julia and Mel! Especially him since the star was brought here by his family. He realized he was starting to feel pride in who he was.

A loud buzzer went off and disturbed David's thoughts. What could that be? David remembered that he had always left with the younger kids after that first bell. This buzzer must signal the time for the grown-ups to go to their church.

Sure enough, the older students and adults left their trays near the kitchen and formed lines. Finally, it was his turn to line up. David pivoted, and without planning to, he looked right into Julia's eyes. Her smile melted the fear gripping his stomach.

"See you inside," she whispered.

"Yeah, see you inside," he said.

David took his pre-assigned place in line and followed the head of his classmate, Johnny Lightly out the side door and up the quiet, dusty path to the church building. Its cold, red brick walls appeared ominous now in contrast to the bright yellow carpeting of children's church.

David wondered about the things Mel and his parents seemed to know but hadn't told him. Did Mr. Aark and Miss Hansen know too? Did the other teachers know things? David looked around at the grownups and felt very alone. He sighed and wondered if Julia felt the same way.

No one spoke out loud. The church bells rang almost rudely, against his thoughts and the solemn tone of the procession. One by one the students followed Miss Hansen into the building. Their heads and bodies disappeared into the darkness beyond the door. David took a deep breath and followed. He saw nothing at first but heard Miss Hansen whisper, "Girls, sit in between the boys,"

Julia's face appeared before him again. She smiled. "David, we can sit together." She squeezed in between David and Johnny. "What a relief!"

"Yes, but isn't it stuffy in here? I feel like I'm suffocating." David tried to open his collar.

"I know." Julia looked up at the ceiling. "There doesn't seem to be any air in here. David looked up too.

As the Bishop began to speak, David looked at him and noticed there was a lit lamp over his head. He poked Julia with his elbow and whispered. "Look at that lamp up there. Is that the 'eternal flame' we read about?"

"You mean the one that the ancient people kept, reminding them of God? Maybe it is." Julia stared at the lamp. "Do you think it will turn into a huge fire, like the one in the basement?"

"I hope so- but look, it's flickering!" David's body tightened and his hands gripped the seat. "It's getting darker in here!" His heart beat wildly and he called out to Julia. "Are you there?"

"Yes". -It was so dark he could not see her.

"Do you see what I see*?" This is getting scary now.*

"What do you see, David?"

"Hardly anything…all the light has gone out of the church."

"That's what I see…nothing."

Shimmering white wings appeared before them. "Evod!" they cried in unison. "Follow me," said Evod. David couldn't tell if the dove spoke out loud or silently like before.

"David, he wants us to follow him again", whispered Julia.

"I heard, but Now? How will we get out of here? We're surrounded by people."

"I don't know, but it's so dark maybe they won't see us leave. It's worth a try."

David looked around for Miss Hansen. He couldn't see her, so he took a moment to hope she couldn't see him either.

Julia's voice broke into his thoughts. "Let's make a run for it."

"Well, ok. I mean we never got in trouble when we were with Evod before." Luckily, there was no one beside David at the end of the pew.

Once in the aisle, light streamed in through a glass door and they could see where they were going. Julia and David raced towards the door. Evod flew through the glass again. Julia reached the door first. She grabbed the handle and pushed. Without looking back, David ran up behind her and they ran through the door before anyone had a chance to stop them. What a miracle! But then again this wasn't the first one!

Evod glided ahead of them, over the front lawn. They ran and laughed.

"I'm so relieved to be out of there, Julia. That was torture."

"Yeah, it was awful! I'm so glad Evod showed up again. Let's go."

Evod led them to the cave they had visited that first day. David had already made up his mind before they got there- he was going to follow Evod no matter what. So, when Evod flew swiftly into the cave, he ran inside.

"David, I hear the music we heard the first day!"

"Me too, but where is it coming from?"

Evod swerved off into a passageway to the right. David and Julia followed. "Where are we going?" panted David.

"I don't know, but Evod does!"

Suddenly, the big dove stopped. They almost ran into the back of him. As David skidded to a stop, he called to Julia, "There's an opening in the rocks."

It was true. At chest height, was a hole in the wall. David, then Julia peeked through it. (What they saw surprised them.) David backed up into Julia

.

The music came from a small compartment. Inside were about two dozen men, singing in perfect harmony, in a language David couldn't fully understand though it was familiar- Each man held a large open scroll with writing like the writing that had wrapped the star. The men did not look at them, or even acknowledge their presence. In fact, most of the men had their eyes closed. As they sang, they swayed back and forth with a look of great peace upon their faces. The men wore long white robes, with blue trim. Blue and white embroidered stars decorated the shawls they wore over their shoulders. Silver candelabras, each with seven white candles, surrounded the men. The blue and white stars were superimposed over everything.

"So that's who was singing. We never found them that day, remember Julia?"

"The stars! Do you see them David?" Julia's voice was full of wonder.

David rubbed his eyes and looked again.

"I sure do. They're just like the star we found. So, these men may be connected to OUR star. He looked at Julia. "Maybe important to the school too."

Julia nodded. "Where did they come from, -the stars and the men?"

Evod's calm voice echoed right through them. "They came from of old."

"Of old? What does that mean?" Julia asked. She looked up at Evod and repeated, "What does that mean?"

"That's what I want to know, too." David addressed the dove as well. "What are you showing us?"

Evod cooed and turned to fly back through the passageway they had just used. David and Julia knew it was their cue to follow him. They looked at each other and shrugged.

Julia sighed, "I don't want to go yet. I want to stay here. I want to find out what they're doing. Maybe we can talk to them-

"I don't think we should try that, but I do want to stay." David turned his head. "Where did Evod go?"

"I'm not leaving. This is awesome. Kind of like the tent, remember?"

"But Julia, we have to leave. We don't know the way back."

"Oh... alright." Julia turned slowly-too slowly for David- and followed him to look for Evod. They found him after they had walked a few feet.

Evod led them back out of the cave and out into the brilliant sunlight.

CHAPTER SIXTEEN
THE TRUTH ABOUT MR. AARK

David and Julia ran behind Evod into a side door of the school. Down a dark hallway for a few minutes and then they both gasped.

They were looking at Mr. Aark! David pushed his body up against the wall so Mr. Aark couldn't see him. Julia did the same. Through a glass window, the principal sat in his office and seemed unaware that he could be seen.

"James Aark closes his door to keep him sealed away from people he thinks are beneath him." Evod said. "He feels he's much too busy to waste his time with unimportant students. He only has time for the rich and famous. He never married—because he thought no one was worthy of him. His only pleasures involve meeting people he could turn into donors for the school. He craves the attention he receives when a wealthy person writes a huge check and his picture is published for all the world to see."

Julia gasped. "Mr. Aark doesn't care about us at all?"

Mr. Aark opened the door and called to Mrs. Barrey. "David Roth and Julia Hingle found a star in the basement. It was that star I told the janitor to throw away! I KNEW that guy was trouble."

David and Julia came to a half wall and hid behind it as they watched the scene. Mrs. Barrey was not more than two feet from them but she didn't have a clue they were there. Evod nestled in the exposed rafters.

"You did say so, Sir," Mrs. Barrey said as her long nails clattered on the keyboard.

Mr. Aark walked into Mrs. Barrey's area and opened a file cabinet. "I wish Mrs. Roth hadn't made me hire him. The Roths…of course." He quickly thumbed through the folders in the cabinet and took one out. He pointed the folder at Mrs. Barrey who was now turned around in her chair, looking at him intently. "Leave it to their own little brat to find it. I don't like those people. They think they're so important, but they're …they're worthless." He started to go back to his office, but turned around, his face red. "Who wants to know about that old star? It's irrelevant. Old Testament stuff."

He wrinkled his nose as if he had smelled a bad odor. "If I could get rid of that infernal star and that family, I would. And all those other old-country people with their weird ways. If the grandfather hadn't made his family part of the school's charter, I would." He shook his head. "

Mrs. Barrey started typing again, then stopped. "They don't have enough money to send David here. They're just phoneys, like all the others in that group."

Mr. Aark looked down at the file folder in his hand.

"But I think I found a way to fix it." A smile spread across his face as he shook the file folder in the air. "Coach said David got into a scuffle with Scotty and Keith in his class. I put him on janitor duty with his friend, Mel. Haha. That should keep him busy and out of MY business." Mr. Aark leaned over at the waist and laughed.

Mrs. Barrey laughed too-a mean, menacing cackle.

"Why can't all families be like Scotty's and Keith's, Mrs. Barrey? We'd keep them."

"And get rid of David and Julia? Huh!" Mrs. Barrey rolled her chair backward. Her large body filled the whole chair. "Well, I'm sure this matter isn't over yet." She looked up at her boss.

"No, David Roth will fail." Mr. Aark smirked and tapped the file folder in his hand. He walked back into his office. "Yes, they're poor now, so it should be easy to break them," he called over his shoulder.

Mrs. Barrey got up and walked away from her desk. David and Julia popped up and started walking briskly down the hallway towards the dining room.

"So that's what's going on." David snarled. "I can't believe it. He not only hates me, but my family and our people."

"David, this is terrible. I feel so bad for you…us." Julia's eyes showed her sympathy. David's dark thoughts were interrupted when Evod spoke again.

Evod turned and faced the children. "Remember, it is your assigned quest to follow the clues of the star. I fly around you sometimes, without you seeing me. You are never alone. I lead all children, grown-ups and treasures such as the star to the place where they belong - to the place where they find out who they really are." Evod faded out.

"Is that some kind of riddle?" David asked, as he turned to Julia. She shrugged. They walked through the dining room and back up into the church. No one seemed to notice them.

Julia elbowed David. "Wow, what was that? My body is tingling like I was just on a roller coaster."

"Me too." David pinched his arm. Yep, he was awake. He hadn't been dreaming. "Did you see the dove-Evod? As soon as I saw him, I wasn't scared at all!"

"Me neither -"

David noticed all the lights were now on in the building "That was weird. And the part about Mr. Aark?" David shuddered. "Should we tell someone?"

Just then, a student near them burst out "Ssh!" David and Julia looked toward their right for Miss Hansen. She was not paying attention to them.

Julia scowled and moved closer to David. "Heck no. Don't tell. That would get us in big trouble. No one would believe us anyway." She shook her long hair. "They would think we're liars and expel us. We better keep it all a secret for now."

David didn't move. He thought for a second and then whispered, "Just between us?"

"Yes."

"Pinky- swear?"

He hooked pinkies with Julia and then looked around, glad no one was watching. He sighed as the organ music ended and the adults filled the aisles. Service was over, and he'd missed it. (He didn't care.) He leaned back in the pew and smiled. He was glad he hadn't missed this adventure with Evod!

CHAPTER SEVENTEEN
THE STAR IS GONE

"What? I don't believe it! Mr. Aark THREW the star OUT?" David stared at Julia in disbelief. "Are you sure? How do you know?"

Julia and David had been the first to arrive in the classroom after lunch.

"David, I was just in there with Ruth getting her science project. The star isn't in the closet."

"…And you asked Mr. Aark about it?" David followed Julia to her desk.

"Yes, I asked him, and he said it cluttered up the closet too much, so he threw it out." Julia sat down and held her head.

"You asked Mrs. Barrey?" David couldn't believe it. "You asked specifically, about the star?"

"Yes, David!"

"He said he was going to keep it safe. He really does hate that star, Julia, like he said." David paced. "But the school needs that star- I'm sure of it now." David clenched his fists and slammed them into each other. "I was right in the first place. We shouldn't have trusted Mr. Aark with the star."

Julia stood up quickly. "I know. I'm sorry. It's

all my fault." David scanned her face as tears popped up in her eyes.

"Maybe he didn't throw it out, but hid it, like before." David said, hoping to cheer Julia.

"Hid? Do you think it's in the basement again?" Julia gazed out the door, toward the stairs.

"I don't know." He kept his hands balled into two tight fists. "First, we need to get into that office to make sure it's not there." He pointed at Julia. "Then check out the basement and anywhere else it could be." David began to pace again.

Julia nodded slowly, deep in thought. "I know my mom sometimes has lunch with Mrs. Barrey. If she can distract her and Mr. Aar----"

Footsteps pounded up the stairs. David saw panic in Julia's eyes even as he felt his heart start to beat through his shirt.

He whispered through his dry throat. "We could try that"—David jetted over to his desk and sat down.

The laughter of his entering classmates only contrasted with the sick feeling in his stomach.

Miss Hansen chirped, "Class, take out your journals." She seemed excited about the assignment she was about to give.

David wasn't.

"This afternoon, we are going to write about something that is important to us. Something that really matters and excites us when we think about it. It can be anything. Open topic."

David flipped through his journal and stared at the first blank page. He drew the star- the same star that was guiding his life now. Above it he wrote

"Evod." He peered behind his back at his classmates, hoping none had seen what he had done. Why did he feel like he was doing something wrong?

Miss Hansen continued. "After you have written about your prized idea or object, you will brainstorm about one step you can take in the next week to pursue that thing."

Her words were drowned out by David's sudden realization that he and Julia could plan a way to steal back the star. They could change the destiny of the school if nothing else went wrong.

CHAPTER EIGHTEEN
EXPLOSION

It was early morning and David's roommates were asleep in their beds. All except David, of course. He wanted to go over his history paper one more time and make sure it was perfect before he turned it into Miss Hansen. Nothing could be out of place-not the spelling, punctuation, or citations. That was the way David did things. He knew he'd have a few minutes during lunch to look at it, but he didn't want to run out of time and hand it in, half-done, or with mistakes.

His alarm buzzed, and David reached over to smack the off button, just as it read 6:30 am. He swung his feet to the floor but when they hit the wooden boards, the planks trembled beneath his feet. The entire room swayed for a moment.

David fell back onto his bed. "What?" David thought someone had fallen in the hallway. He struggled upright and opened his door to check, but no one was there.

Soon the other students emerged from their rooms, too, rubbing their eyes and mumbling, "What was that?"

Through the hall window, David saw Mel scurrying outside. He was holding a flashlight and looking at the foundation of the building. David later learned that there was no damage to the buildings at NCA, so there was no need for evacuation.

Five minutes later, sirens began to scream from the closest town two miles away. Then more sirens and more. They seemed to be coming from all directions- North, South, East and West. What happened? A car wreck? A plane crash?

David rushed back to his bedside and turned on the radio. Just the regular banter from KJJY, local news of Council meetings and the scores of last night's basketball game against the Rockets. His roommates started to stir.

"What's going on?" Buzz rubbed his eyes.

"I don't know," replied David. "The building was shaking! Really shaking!"

David demonstrated with his hands. "And then I heard sirens - didn't you hear them? I'm trying to figure out what happened."

Rolley jumped out of bed and sat on the floor beside David's bed.

They all froze and waited to hear something about what just happened, and sure enough, the announcer burst in with excitement and fear in his voice. "This just in…there seems to have been some kind of explosion at the American School."

The boys stared at each other.

"Whoa!" said Rolley.

"That's incredible," said Buzz.

David sat quietly. He couldn't think of anything to say. The announcer continued as a thick silence settled over the room. "Witnesses said they saw something falling from the sky…We will give you more updates as they become available."

The American School was located on the same row as Naples Christian Academy. It catered to the sons and daughters of famous celebrities and produced successful sports teams. That's why it felt so close. David was ashamed of the next few thoughts he had. *The American School is our rival. They are so proud that they have more money than us. Those snobs, that will show them.*

David looked at his roommates and his heart softened. "What about the kids?" Buzz and Rolley shook their heads. "I hope no one was hurt. Johnny Jones goes there. He was a neighbor of mine at the farm. I haven't seen him for a long time. Tommy and Kenny Pritcher also go there. I hope my friends are okay."

"Yeah –" Rolley chimed in. "I know kids that go there too!"

"Me too," said Buzz.

"Maybe we should pray,"-suggested Rolley. "This IS a Christian School. You pray, David."

"Me?" David felt inadequate. "Well, okay. Oh God, please send help.*"*

"Amen-" said Rolley.

"Amen", said Buzz.

The boys stared at each other—and then got up. They dressed quickly, but silently and Buzz opened the door. He and Rolley ran out. Students poured into the hallway leading to the Great Room.

Julia ran up to David. "David, did you hear? An explosion at the American School!" She grabbed

David's jacket and cried, "My mom's best friend, Sally, works at the American School - I hope everybody is okay over there!"

David nodded silently. Searching for any kind of answer, David said, "Maybe we can watch the TV in the Great Room and find out more." It seemed all the students and teachers had the same idea.

As they started to crowd into the Great Room, Julia whispered. "I feel weird."

"Me too." David was feeling disconnected from the world - a little dizzy, and the objects in front of him looked vague and far away, not sharp and clear as they always did.

"This is surreal. I wonder where Evod is?" David looked around as if he expected to see the great white bird inside the building. "We need him now. Maybe he could show us what is going on. He seems to know the deep things."

The news footage showed that the explosion left The American School in shambles. A voice proclaimed over the video, "Everyone was accounted for. Fortunately, the students and staff were all in their dormitories when the school building was hit. The principal, Mr. McTavish had been safe in his home."

A news reporter appeared in a tan trench coat, his name Guy Green emblazoned across the bottom of the screen.

"Ladies and gentlemen, here is the builder of the American School, Mr. Solomon Strumpstein."

"The school was built to code in the 1950s but could not withstand whatever this was. I am sad to see the damage, but I'm sure it was not a design error as some have suggested. It was a bomb of some sort."

The man wagged his finger at the camera. "We need to get to the bottom of this. These youngsters have been traumatized and should never have been in danger. I am looking forward to the FBI investigating this disaster…"

"Thank you very much, Mr. Strumpstein" the reporter cut him off and the screen went blank for a moment. Then the news continued with a story about the US Postal Service.

Julia turned to David. "What will the school do without classrooms?"

"I don't know," David responded, then turned toward his teacher. "Miss Hansen, what will The American School do without classrooms?" Miss Hansen put her finger to her lips and said nothing. She leaned against the wall, looking very pale.

School began one hour late that day. Everything was a blur. David sensed a fearful cloud was lingering over the school. The teachers and students seemed nervous and afraid. No one spoke much, and the students couldn't concentrate on their studies.

Despite the gloom, David searched the sky for Evod, and thought of ways to leave the classroom to look for him. He dropped his pencil in front of Julia's desk, leaned over to get it and whispered, "We've got to find Evod. Maybe he's in the field. Let's look at recess."

"Okay, David," Julia whispered. She kept her eyes on the teacher as she nodded. When they went outside, however, there was no sign of their friend. The teachers circled the children and didn't let them out of their sight. David and Julia couldn't explore the field, as they had hoped.

CHAPTER NINETEEN
AFTERMATH

David held his hands over his ears to shut out the clamor of his classmate's curiosity. "Was it a bomb or weapon of war? Fireworks?"

"Or was it just a pipe exploding?"

It had been a long day of questions. David wanted his parents. No one had any answers. Not even Miss Hansen.

The week dragged on, and David could feel the atmosphere at the school was filled with worry and fear. Every loud noise made the students jump. The teachers got aggravated when David or the other students asked questions. There were a lot of students sent to the office, and the noise of teachers yelling.

By Thursday, some details had emerged.

"My dad said it was just a pipe exploding." Scotty said, as he turned in all directions from his seat to make sure they'd all heard him. "Nothing to worry about." "That possibility was ruled out early in the investigation," reported Hannah Snipes, the class know-it-all. "The furnace and pipes had recently been inspected."

McKenzie Dillard, whose father worked for the government spoke up. "My dad said the government is sending lots of investigators. No answers yet. One person called and said they were an eyewitness. They said they saw a plane overhead, and even sketched a picture, but it was never found. In fact, my dad doesn't even think it exists -there is no such plane in existence!"

Everyone moaned.

At lunch that day, Julia confided in David. "My stomach is in a knot! I try to eat breakfast, but I can't. And I'm not the only one. The breakfast tables are strewn with half-full bowls of oatmeal and half-eaten bagels all week. And lunch isn't any better." She turned her head sideways toward David and put her hand in front of her mouth so no one could hear her. "Every day my stomach is finally calm around 10:00 a.m. I feel really hungry then, but of course, there's no food at that time." She stared at the banana in front of her. "By 11:30, my stomach is usually in a knot again, and nothing looks good now, not the salads, sandwiches and not even the brownies."

David chuckled, "The boys seem to be eating even more than ever. I think the grownups are probably happy some kids aren't eating." He took a bite of his apple.

Julia swiped David's arm. "It's not funny, David...hey by the way, I was thinking..." she whispered through clenched teeth, "Now's the time to look for the star. Nobody is paying attention and we can sneak into Mr. Aark's office."

"Are you crazy, Julia?" David pulled his arm away. "We've already been in detention for being where we weren't supposed to be! Our schools are under attack. They may even suspect us for all we know. It would really look bad if they caught us breaking into the principal's office!"

Julia was insistent. "All the more reason we have to find the star. It might have something to do with solving the crime!"

"IF there's a crime."

David shook his head, dumped his tray and started walking back to class. Julia came up behind him. "Who do you think blew up the school? Was it an angry student... a parent... or a teacher?"

"Or an outsider?"

Julia recoiled when he said that, and immediately David was sorry he had. He cleared his throat and tried again. "I didn't mean you, Julia." He waited a beat. "Now, if it had been angry students, how could they have pulled it off?"

Julia seemed to brush off David's earlier comment. "And all these questions lead to why? What benefit could anyone get from bombing a boarding school way out in the middle of nowhere?"

David answered, "I don't know. I really don't." Before he realized what was happening, David found himself silently following Julia down the hallway towards Mr. Aark's office. He wanted to pull back and go the other way, but they were almost there. When they rounded the last corner, Julia and David saw yellow "crime scene" tape all around the Administration Office. Policemen mingled here and there, carrying tablets, notebooks, pencils and most notably, guns tucked in holsters mounted on their sides.

"What's going on?" David demanded loudly. His boldness took him by surprise. Julia ducked behind him.

"I'd like to ask you the same thing, young man." growled a policeman. His puffy white face with red nose pushed right up against David's face. "You need to get away from these premises ASAP."

Julia lunged backward, pulling on the back of David's navy jacket. "Come on, let's go."

"Good idea!" the policeman shouted at them.

They ran down the hall and to the safety of the cafeteria. After a few minutes in the chaos of students wandering around and not eating, Julia said, "Let's go see my mom."

David nodded. His stomach felt queasy now too. David slowly followed Julia at a distance and sat in the admitting area as Julia went to talk to her mother. He played with the gummy soles of his shoes.

Julia ran out "David! Mr. Aark is a suspect!"

"What?" David stood up abruptly and hit his head on a display case screwed on the wall. Rubbing the back of his head, he looked at her in disbelief. "That's not funny, Julia."

"I'm not joking, David!" Julia stood with her feet apart and glared at him. Then she put her fists together and bounced up and down. "He's been arrested. My mom saw it!"

David didn't like Mr. Aark, but ...he wouldn't bomb another school, would he? David looked down and shook his head "That explains the police." he mumbled.

"David, the local police station received a phone

call after the blast, saying that Mr. Aark was seen leaving the American School that morning!" She looked up and took a breath. "And now they say Mr. Aark had been writing nasty emails to the principal of The American

School. In fact, one email threatened "dire circumstances" if The American School did not share some money with Naples."

"Money? What money?" David felt overwhelmed.

"My mom said a lot of money had been bequeathed, or given, to both schools - Naples and The American School - by a rich man. The two schools were supposed to share it, but it looks like The American School took all the money."

David took a step. He felt drained. "This is all just ...too big for us... I sure wish Evod would show us what is going on."

After dark that night, David searched the skies for Evod. He and Julia had managed to lose the star, and the American School had been destroyed. Their principal disliked them and now was a suspect. What else could go wrong and jangle his nerves? "Evod, please come and help!" he cried out into the darkness.

CHAPTER TWENTY
THE WAR

"Students, students, calm down," Dorm Master Robbins (now called Headmaster Robbins) yelled from the stage. Shortly after the morning bell Mrs. Hansen had lined them up and ushered them into the auditorium for an impromptu assembly. "I know you are wondering what is going to happen now, since The American School has been damaged. It has been decided that most students from there will attend Naples Christian Academy."

"Oh, no," David's classmates groaned.

Rolley spoke into David's ear. "Not those snobs! Coming here? They are always bragging about how rich they are. They can't come here!"

David covered his ears and looked around the auditorium. A lot of angry faces, and angry voices came from every direction.

"Oh no. Not here! They'll ruin everything.'

"I'm going to tell my parents. They will complain to the Board."

Mr. Robbins ignored the outbursts. "Since there is not enough room for two full schools to merge into one, it has been decided that only the lower grades,

K-5 will transfer to Naples. Grades 6 through High School will be distributed among the other prep schools; The French Academy, The British Academy and the New Zealand School."

More groaning.

"It's just not fair." David looked at Julia. She looked just as puzzled as he felt.

"I don't know what this means, Julia."

"Neither do I. I'll ask my mom." She looked around the packed room. "As soon as I get the chance, I'll ask Miss Hansen to send me to her office. Mom will know."

"That's a good idea, Julia." David sat straighter in his seat. "That makes me feel better."

From the stage, Mr. Robbins boomed, "Ladies and Gentlemen, that's it for now." Ignoring the questions and protests, he continued. "You are excused. Please follow your teachers back to class."

Miss Hansen was abrupt when they all returned to the classroom. "Let's get to work." She launched into the math lesson, with no time for questions.

***

"I feel like I'm in a war zone," David told Julia as they walked back from class together a few weeks after the arrival of the students from The American School. "'Psychological warfare', my dad said last night on the phone. He said to be strong and courageous and not give in to fear."

David stopped and looked around. "Have you noticed the kids from The American School are skittish and quiet?"

"They have good reason to be afraid, David."

"I know —but everyone here at Naples-" David

gestured at the students around them. "is nervous too, wondering if this school will be next. That includes the students AND the teachers."

"That's true." Julia grimaced at the students rushing by her and swung her backpack to her shoulder. "Ever since Headmaster Robbins took over for Mr. Aark, things have been different." She pointed at her dormitory. "Like that guard at the front door, and more and more police cars showing up on the street near the school." She looked at David. "Remember when Headmaster Robbins came on the intercom that first day after Mr. Aark's arrest and said, 'Boys and girls and teachers, we must change the way we think?'"

David nodded. "That was creepy." He lowered his voice. "And almost every day after that, the classroom speakers boom out the same message: 'Change, change, change. Due to the recent bombing, we will have no milk, we will have no outdoor recess today, all cats and Children of the Star will be inspected at the office.'" He laughed. "That last one I made up, but you know what I mean."

Julia smiled weakly. "Yes, I don't like the suspicious looks when we walk down the hall. What's up with that, David?" She moved closer and said, "And the whispering and pointing when we talk in class? I feel so uncomfortable, like kids are spying on us or something."

She and David left the sidewalk and walked across the lawn, away from the throngs of students leaving the main classroom building. Julia went on. "I feel like the kids from the families who have been here for years are not stared at; I bet they sleep nice and sound in their beds every night. Not me."

They stopped at a bench and David put his foot on the seat. "They've always been Mr. Aark's favorites and now they are Headmaster Robbins' favorites." Julia sat down on the bench and rifled through her backpack.

David shook his head. "I only know the teachers look tense, and you can feel the fear during the day. PE's been changed to indoor only, so with little exercise and bad eating habits, kids are getting sick."

Julia pulled a sneaker out and held it up to David. He shrugged and she put it back into her backpack. "Kids are wanting their parents more than ever. I even heard the littler ones were crying, sucking their thumbs and wetting their pants more than usual." She had to stifle a laugh, but then looked at David and furrowed her eyebrows.

David sighed. "My dad said we have to stay at the school. We won't be able to go home for at least four weeks!" Tension rose in his voice. "The only good thing in my life besides talking with you is when my mom calls once a week. It feels good while I'm on the phone with her, as if nothing is wrong." He stopped and smiled for a few seconds.

"I'm glad my mom works here," said Julia.

"You're lucky." David brushed a tear from his eye. He hoped Julia didn't notice. "I can only talk to my mom on the phone." He spoke faster. "But one night, she asked to talk to Miss Hansen on the old-fashioned phone in the main hallway. I could hear them."

"You could, David? What did they say?"

"Mom said, 'I'm so afraid. Do you think he should come home?'"

"Miss Hansen said, 'No, you know the governor thinks your town might be next. He'll be safe here. I'll make sure of that."

"Wow, she said that, David?"

"Yeah, do you believe it?"

They started walking again. Julia laughed. "Miss Hansen is actually turning out to be human. She seems much kinder in class, and she even began visiting us in the girls' dorm, hugging us at bedtime."

"I know, Julia." David looked to the sky and spread out his hands. "I can't believe it. When I told her I had trouble sleeping, she began reading us stories at night. At first, I thought her stories were babyish, but they did help me calm down and get to sleep."

"Stories? What kind of stories, David?" Julia walked closer to David.

"Well, one story was about a lamb being taken care of by its owner. The lamb didn't need anything; the shepherd took care of all its needs. He gave it nice green grass, and he even prepared a place for the lamb to lay down and rest." David swiped another tear away. "He led the lamb all over."

"Like Mary had a little lamb?" Julia asked.

David chuckled. "Yeah, I guess. The shepherd would pick up the lamb if it got tired and spank the lamb gently if it was naughty! There was plenty of food for the little lamb. A whole picnic table was spread out with the lamb's favorite foods in fact: clover and sugar and honey, and even corn, ice cream and pie."

"Wow, that sounds nice," Julia broke in.

"Yeah and listen to this. The owner poured sweet, good-smelling oil all over the lamb to protect it from bugs and mosquitoes. The oil showed that the lamb was special to the shepherd. He also gave the lamb courage and strength to go on."

"What else, David?" Julia seemed calmer now, and David was happy to

oblige her by telling more.

"Well -as the little lamb walked on, he saw two angels following him, making sure he was safe. The lamb always wanted to be with his owner, and that special owner was going to let that lamb stay under his care forever." David sighed. "After that, when Miss Hansen left, I felt a sweet feeling, and I slept all the way until morning. Sometimes I dream about the lamb and shepherd. And sometimes I dream about the Kingdom of the Star."

"You're still having those dreams? About the King and all that?" David nodded, lost in thought.

"Oh, I'm not. I'm having nightmares." She looked down and shivered. "Mostly about the bombing if that was what it was. I'm really scared."

Both of them were silent as they walked. When they got to the door of her dorm building, Julia stopped and smiled. "But once, I did have a dream about Evod though."

"You did, really? You didn't tell me." David stopped and stared at her. "What happened in the dream?"

"Well, we were inside the classroom, like the first day. Evod showed up outside and tried to tell us who blew up the school." Julia looked intently into David's eyes. "He knows who blew up the school, David. I could just tell from the dream. It was so real."

David shook his head sadly. "I wish we could see him flying around. I would feel so much better."

Julia grabbed David's lapels and said excitedly. "David, I think it's true. Remember, he told us he was!" David's eyes grew big as he remembered. "He's watching us. Even though I don't see him, at the oddest times, I think I feel his presence. First a thrill runs through my body, then a calm feeling." She rubbed her forearms. "It's like he's trying to tell us we're not alone."

David was glad Julia had said that. He had to admit that was his hope as well. "I feel it too, Julia. I really do."

CHAPTER TWENTY-ONE
DISCOVERIES

"Students," Miss Hansen said, "It is time for us to discuss what happened at the American School." Several students sighed.

Finally.

David looked around at the worried faces. Maybe they'd get some answers. Julia fidgeted in her chair.

Miss Hansen began slowly. "We know that there was some type of explosion... We know Mr. Aark…is not here. We don't know the full extent of the investigation, but we do know we need to stand behind Mr. Aark until we know for sure if, and that's a big if, he was actually involved in this terrible crime. He is innocent until proven guilty."

Questions bombarded her from all directions, all at the same time. Miss Hansen put out her palm towards them, to try and quell the anxiety that could be felt in the classroom. "Everything will be alright. The police are taking care of everything and protecting us." She looked around the room at the distressed faces. "That's all I can say on the matter. Let's get back to work," she said firmly.

Later, at lunch outside, David asked Julia, "Do you think the new kids are jealous of the Naples students?"

Julia looked up from her sandwich. "They could be…Well, first of all, we haven't gone through the terror of an explosion, like they have. And our school isn't damaged."

David handed her some chips. "Yeah, the Naples kids haven't been asked to leave what's familiar and start all over again at a new place. I feel sorry for the new kids."

Julia wrinkled her nose. "But those kids stick together and don't talk to any of us. I tried to be friendly, but it seems like whatever I say or do, it's not enough."

David and Julia gathered up their trash, and Julia looked away as JJ (Johnny Jones) walked over. He was the friend David had worried about on that terrible morning. He jumped up and gave JJ an awkward hug. JJ had transferred from The American School, but David had known him for a longtime.

"Hey dude, glad to see you," David laughed. "I see you are in one piece."

"Yeah," said JJ, holding out his hand with thumb pulled back. "Good to see you too, Dave." He smiled and looked around. "How can you stand this boring school? And the food, yuck!"

David didn't introduce Julia to JJ, so after a few minutes of awkward silence, Julia left. JJ wasted no time in recruiting David for some mischief. "Hey, David. Do you want to go to the American School with me tonight and snoop around? It could be fun."

David was surprised, but only a little. JJ always

found ways to get into trouble. "The American School? Your old school? The one that was bombed or something?" David really didn't want to do it, at least not at first. "Naw, JJ that sounds dangerous. And wouldn't we get in trouble?"

"Come on David, you're not *chicken*, are you?" JJ seemed to be smirking. David hated that. "The other guys are going."

"I'm not chicken!" David's face grew hot.

"Oh yeah? Then why won't you come?"

David looked away from JJ's freckled face. *JJ is so excited. Why shouldn't I go?* David asked himself. *I'm tired of waiting for Evod to show up. It's time for some excitement for me!* "Ok, JJ, when?" said David, halfway hoping JJ was bluffing.

"Tonight, after dinner. I'll come get you." JJ slapped David on the back.

David winced. "Sure," he heard himself say. But inside he was starting to feel queasy. That night— however, after dinner, J.J. and David snuck down the fire escape of their dorm. It was still light outside, so they were taking some risk that they would be seen, but that added to the excitement.

To David's surprise, when they got there, they saw most of the fifth grade scattered across the crime scene. *This must be okay,* he thought. *All these kids are here. I'll just blend in.*

The students were all standing on mounds of dirt and ash, digging through the rubble which had not been completely removed. David and JJ quickly ducked under the yellow tape and got to work, chatting and laughing as they explored.

"Hey, David. I'll go over this way. You try that

pile over there. See if you can find any cool stuff," JJ said.

The gray ash was terrible. It rose with each shift of his feet. It clung to his face and turned his hand gray. David coughed, but the other boys didn't mind the inconvenience, for the adventure. After about ten minutes, JJ called out from the midst of the mess, "Hey, look what I found!"

David stopped digging and looked over at JJ. A wave of nausea swept from his stomach to the top of his head when he saw what JJ held up in his hand.

It was the star, HIS star. David dropped the broken pieces of pottery he was holding and ran over to JJ. It felt like his legs were in slow motion. "Give me that," he yelled.

"Oh no you don't! I found it first!" JJ tried to shove the star inside his coat.

David reached out to grab the star. "But I found it first at my school . . . and—" David stopped. As soon as the words had come out of his mouth, he was sorry.

JJ looked at David. "Sure, you did." JJ laughed loudly. "I don't believe you."

The other boys were far away and only a few heads turned toward them. David waited until they turned away and went on with their own exploring.

He reached for the star again. JJ held it tight. They pulled and tugged. David dug his feet into the ash covered earth.

"Let go!" JJ yelled. "I found it."

"It's mine!"

As they pulled, and pushed, the star released into David's hand. He tumbled backward and fell to the ground. He held up the star - half the star - one of the two large triangles.

"Look what you did, you idiot!" screamed David.

Hot tears rolled down David's face.

JJ leaned over him. "I'm sorry, David. I didn't think it would break," he said. He put his half of the star next to David's. "Maybe we can glue it."

Immediately, the star filled up with heat and light. When the two pieces touched, they fused back together!

"Hey! Did you see that? How did it do that?" asked JJ, "Hey, you said you found this star before? What do you know about it?" He sat down next to David in the dirt pile.

David pressed his lips together and examined the places of the fracture. There was no sign of any damage. He told the star, *I'm so glad I found you again- and you really ARE supernatural.*

David quietly told JJ what he and Julia had discovered about the star before he could stop himself. From that time on, David and JJ formed a bond, and spent more time together. Julia noticed, and was skeptical of their friendship and even a little jealous. So, she was glad when David asked her to meet him behind the bleachers a few days later.

"Oh, Julia, you won't believe it, I found the star." David reached into his bag and pulled it out.

Julia gasped, and then her face lit up.

David continued. "We went over to the American School and found it in the dirt. It got broken, but I saw it put itself back together! Isn't that cool?"

Julia sat down next to David and admired the star.

"I-I didn't know it could do that. Are you serious, David?"

"Yes. Remember how it was hot in our hands when we first found it?"

"I do remember." She lifted her gaze from the star and looked at David. "Wait, you said we. Who is we?"

"Well, I mean, actually JJ found it, and...-"

"JJ? HE found it?" Julia's face got red. "Does this mean JJ knows about the star?" She thrust the star back to David and stood up.

"Of course, Julia."

Julia put her hands on her hips. "David, you shouldn't have told him anything. He might tell, and we will all get in trouble. Besides, I don't trust him – he has beady eyes!" she scolded.

David laughed. "Well, I guess his beady eyes came in handy. He found this, didn't he?" David tucked the star into his backpack and looked up at Julia. "We couldn't find it. Let's give him a chance."

"I can't believe you kept this from me! How long have you had the star?"

"Just since Tuesday night."

"Tuesday night? Today is Thursday! Are you and JJ going on adventures without me?"

"Julia, Julia, don't worry. JJ doesn't know anything about Evod or those adventures. He just knows about the star, that's all."

Julia sighed and looked down. "Well, I guess that's okay." She looked at David earnestly. "But no more secrets, okay? Not even for a few days."

"You got it partner." They both laughed.

CHAPTER TWENTY-TWO
MISS HANSEN

"Well, we know it has supernatural powers."
David paced the corner of the hallway afterschool.
Now that they had possession of the star, they needed
to decide what to do with it. "We could give it to
Mel."

Julia sat cradling the star. "No, David, Mel said
we have to figure it out. Remember?"

"I have an idea." JJ held up his finger. "How
about Miss Hansen? She's a teacher after all. She
knows how to look stuff up. The star is safe now
since Mr. Aark is in jail. You said he's the one who
lost it- or got rid of it. But Miss Hansen wouldn't."

"I think JJ has a point," David said.

Julia moaned. "But, David, how can we trust
her? She's just another adult who probably won't
even think the star is important. She could throw it
out, too."

"Not if we explain it to her, Julia."

"I'm still not convinced." Julia gazed at the star
"Wait, what about your parents, David?"

"Well, now you're making sense." David
grinned. "I'll ask them this weekend."

David's parents did not want to keep the star at their house. They repeatedly insisted that it belonged at the school. They threatened to take it there themselves. Then David told them about JJ's idea. They thought Miss Hansen was the logical choice.

On Monday, the three kids met again and finally agreed. They decided to go to their teacher after school and give her the star. David and JJ said they trusted her and convinced Julia this was the best course of action.

"What is that?" asked Miss Hansen as David approached her with the star.

"It's a special star, Miss Hansen." said David. He thought he saw Miss Hansen back away a few steps as he came closer. She stood with her hand on the bookshelf labeled HISTORY/RESEARCH.

"Why did you bring it here?" She glanced around the room.

"We brought it here because we thought you could help us find out what it is and why it was here at the school," David said.

"It was at the school? Where?" Miss Hansen looked afraid.

"That really doesn't matter." said Julia from her place behind the boys.

"It might have to do with the bombing, or explosion or whatever it was...and Mr. Aark."

"And how do you know that?" The teacher put her hand on her chest.

Julia continued. "It was found at the American School. David and JJ found it there. Someone must have left it. We don't know who."

"You went to the American School?" Miss

Hansen stared at the boys. "You know that is against the rules we set up for your safety."

"We know, and we're sorry-" David answered. "But did you know most of the class and lots of other kids are going over there?"

"With the police surveillance? That's ridiculous!" She picked up her phone to call someone.

"Will you help us, Miss Hansen?" David moved quickly towards her and looked purposefully into her eyes. She stopped and looked at him.

"Help you? David, I can't help you." She shook her head. "This is a criminal matter. And now you have interfered. Do you understand? You could be in a lot of trouble."

"Well yes," David conceded. "But I know this is a special star. It came from my great-grandfather, didn't it?" Miss Hansen stared at him blankly. He continued. "My parents said it has to do with the starting of the school…and bringing the star and the cross together." Miss Hansen didn't reply. "So, you see we've just got to have it here, Miss Hansen. My parents said it would be safest with you, because, well, they trust you. Will you help us?" David searched her eyes for a "yes".

"Your parents…said that? Well, I was told about a star that was here, but later it was forbidden for some reason." She looked down. "I've always been curious why…" Looking at the children's innocent faces, she softened. "Of course, I will help you."

David felt so relieved. He continued, "Then please take this and take good care of it. I know this is a big thing, maybe even dangerous, but the star has special powers. It's indestructible." (He grinned at JJ.) He handed the star to her.

Julia chimed in. "We gave it to Mr. Aark before the bombing. Actually, right after we gave it to him, it disappeared. Then the bombing happened."

Miss Hansen looked at Julia, then at the star in her right hand. "Well, I'm concerned about having this responsibility, but I truly care about you. I will do what I can. I'll start with these reference books right here."

David and Julia sighed with relief as they turned to leave. They and JJ could rest easy. Their teacher had the star. Maybe she would teach them all about it. With Mr. Aark in jail, that seemed likely.

***

After the kids left, Miss Hansen walked to a Reading table with the star and sat down. She stared at it for a long time, and then put her face in her hands.

Mary Louise Hansen was a very timid woman. If you saw her in a crowd of people, she would be hiding in the back. She didn't speak up to anyone – not her family, the staff, or Mr. Aark - even when she thought they were wrong. She was too afraid. And now, all alone in her classroom, she felt afraid again. *What am I supposed to do with this glass star? A star that might have caused a bombing at a school. This is too big for me!*

Then she thought of all the times she was afraid as a little girl. Her mother would read her those stories out of the book that would calm her, just like she did with David and the other children. The stories were about being watched over and protected. So, right then and there, Miss Hansen decided to fold her hands like she did when she was a little child and ask for help. As she started to close her eyes, she thought she saw a large white bird fly by her window.

CHAPTER TWENTY-FOUR
CLASSROOM FLOOD

The sun shone brightly as David and Julia walked to class together. They went up the steps to the Science Building and David felt happy and free. Miss Hansen would take care of the star, his parents would be satisfied, and Julia and JJ were now good friends of his.

The other students were seated along laboratory tables when David and Julia arrived.

Mr. Breed was assigning partners. Julia and David scurried to some empty stools. Mr. Breed nodded towards them and cleared his throat.

"You two may as well be partners." He then began reading the lists of supplies each pair would need.

Out of the corner of his left eye, David saw a flash of light. He turned toward the window and saw a glimmer. "Won't you open up ye ancient doors and the windows? So the King's Glory can come in?"

Was it Evod? It sounded like him! David jumped to his feet and craned his neck to look out the window.

Jason Steens - a student sitting to the left of Julia, hopped up and opened the latch.

A low roar rumbled from outside the window. All heads turned toward the window and an arm of fresh water rushed into the room. It swirled around the legs of the stools. Instead of being afraid, David and his classmates were delighted.

The teacher tried desperately to call out instructions, but what could he say? They were on the 2nd floor of an old building, and a torrent of water had just rushed in.

The water climbed until it reached the level of the seats. It lifted each student off their seats and carried them around the room, willy-nilly. Smiles were on the faces of each one.

David found himself laughing and giggling in the gentle water. JJ floated over to Julia and helped her stay upright. She smiled at him. David was lying on his back, floating, and completely relaxed. The other kids were relaxed too.

Just as quickly as it had come, the water receded and the kids were on the floor, laughing uncontrollably. Julia, JJ and David looked at each other, trying to stop, but they couldn't stop laughing.

"Now, everyone please stand up…Uh, stand up if you can…uh, try to stand up." Mr. Breed slipped around on the wet floor and then began to laugh uncontrollably as well.

Teachers from down the hall raced in, having heard the commotion. "What is going on here?" demanded another science teacher.

"I don't know" said Mr. Breed, in between

chuckles. "I don't know what happened, but we're all fine…we're more than fine.". He started laughing again "But…I didn't do it, really I didn't, ha ha, hee, hee."

"Well, you'd better stop it," she said, with a sour look around the room. "Or I'll tell the administration!"

David looked around. Where had Evod gone?

CHAPTER TWENTY-FIVE
BETRAYAL

"I don't know what happened, Class, I don't know." Mr. Breed laughed. "Wasn't it great, though? I truly felt free."

"So did I!" exclaimed Jason Steens.

"Me, too" echoed another voice, and another and another.

"Kids, let's not tell anyone anything about this yet. We wouldn't want your parents to worry. I will research this phenomenon and tell you what I find out next week when we meet again." He smiled and looked like he knew a secret. The students around his desk giggled and followed him into his office next door.

"Did you see Evod, Julia?" David whispered as he tried to get up off the floor.

"I sure did!" Julia's eyes were beaming. She jumped up and looked around. "But I don't see him now."

David hurried to the window. "Me neither. I hope he's outside." He walked back to Julia. "I think I'll go to Miss Hansen's classroom. I want to check on the star."

"Okay," said Julia. "I'm going back to my dorm and change out of my wet clothes. I don't want my roommates to see, -they will never believe what just happened." She started for the stairs.

She turned back and said to David, "You know, JJ isn't so bad after all. He helped me in the water today."

David grinned. "What did I tell you?"

Julia trotted down the stairs.

David called after her, "Don't forget what Mr. Breed said. We'd better not tell anyone yet, especially since we know more than everyone else."

David walked down the stairs alone, thinking about all that had just taken place. Evod had taken the whole class and Mr. Breed on an adventure! Would they have to share Evod with the others now? Why? What did the water mean? When David got to the bottom of the stairs and looked outside, he forgot all about being wet. He saw Evod.

This time Evod seemed to be following him. David smiled. A sense of peace and protection enveloped him all the way from the Science Building to the Intermediate Grade Building. The dove stayed outside as he walked upstairs and right up to Miss Hansen's desk in

the empty classroom.

"Hello, David. How can I help you?" Miss Hansen looked up with a smile. "You're all wet!"

David thought fast. "Sprinklers."

Miss Hansen nodded.

"Well, I wanted to check on the star."

"The star. Oh, yes." Miss Hansen scooted her chair back and stood up. "A wonderful thing happened David. I was able to sell the star and get Mr. Aark out of jail. Isn't that marvelous?"

David stared at her in disbelief. "You...you didn't. You promised to keep it, and research it...and...and protect it!"

"There's no need to raise your voice David. Let me tell you what happened."

David sat down on a desk and tried to stay calm as Miss Hansen continued.

"I decided to go see Mr. Aark in jail. First, I asked him if he did it. Mr. Aark said no, he thought he was set up..."

"Yeah, sure."

Miss Hansen sat on a desk opposite David. He could tell she was trying to calm him down. Like grownups do when they want to make you understand something, but you just end up feeling small.

"I asked him about the star," continued Miss Hansen. "He did have it with him. He wondered how I knew about it. I decided to say, "Let's just say a little birdie told me." She winked at David. "I didn't want to get you and the others in trouble."

David couldn't get himself to smile back at Miss Hansen. She continued. "Mr. Aark believes someone saw him leaving the school in his car right before the explosion. That's why he is a suspect. He also said there were two men in Mr. McTavish's office that day, suspicious looking characters."

Miss Hansen's usual reserved expression changed as she opened her eyes wide. "Well, David,

I was shocked. I asked Mr. Aark, 'That's odd. At a school? Around students?' Mr. Aark said at the time it alarmed him, but as the day unfolded with the explosion, and him getting arrested…. he completely forgot about those men."

Miss Hansen took a sip of water.

David stood up and tapped his foot. He crossed his arms.

Miss Hansen looked at David. "The papers made it sound like Mr. Aark was the only stranger at the school that day, David. Now it appears that's not true. I asked him what his bail was, and he said $50,000! He cried about missing his students. Oh, he was so pitiful, David!"

David did not have any pity in his heart for Mr. Aark. He looked down.

Moving to the window, she continued, "On my way out of the jail, I stopped at the front desk. I asked about Mr. Aark's bail. They told me where and how to pay it."

Miss Hansen paced. "I didn't have $50,000 and I knew the school didn't." She rung her hands. "Then I remembered the star. I looked it up online and saw that it was worth at least $50,000. The next day, I went to a little glass shop in the downtown area."

She began pacing again. "When I got there, the Austrian blinds were up, and the sun reflected wildly around the glass artifacts in the shop. Rainbows here, rainbows there. It was beautiful!"

David grimaced with impatience. He sat down at another desk near the front of the room.

Miss Hansen followed him. "An elderly woman greeted me. I asked for an appraisal on the star. She couldn't give it to me but said her husband, Mr. Humsfeffer could."

Miss Hansen took another sip of water and straightened her skirt. "Well, David, I didn't feel comfortable leaving the star there. I didn't fully trust the lady, even though she had very kind eyes."

David couldn't bear the suspense anymore. "And...so you DIDN'T leave it there?"

"No, not at that time."

David sighed. "Well, where is it then? When did Mr., er Hum…"

"Humsfeffer," Miss Hansen interjected.

"Does he have it now?"

"I had found out it was a special, rare Mogen David star worth $50,000. And while we were talking, I noticed the star began to glow."

"I told you, Miss Hansen, it has some kind of power!"

Miss Hansen stood in front of David again and smiled kindly. "Yes, it does, David. I believe you...Well, the man didn't want to give me the right price, but after a while he said, 'You got me, I see from the details that this is the Mogen David Star. I can give you $35,000." I countered, $50,000. He finally gave in. So, I got the money and took it to the police station and Mr. Aark is now free!"

David jumped to his feet. He put his hands on his hips and stomped his foot. "You promised! You said you would take care of it!"

"I know, David, but-"

"No! You promised! I can't believe you sold the star! That star is important. More important than rotten old Mr. Aark!"

"I can still help."

David shook his head and put up his hand. "No." He gulped a deep breath.

"Do you have the number for the glass store Miss Hansen, or a card? Maybe it's not too late to get the star back. We could bring it back to the school."

"No, David. The star has been sold. Don't you want Mr. Aark out on bail? Maybe he

can help solve the crime of who bombed the school."

"Mr. Aark won't help. He hates the star. I know he does." David felt his face getting hot. "Please, Ms. Hansen, the card. Like I told you, the star is important."

"David, you said the star was important to solving the crime. And I proved it. I got Mr.

Aark out of jail with it."

"You got him out of jail, but you didn't solve anything! You weren't supposed to SELL it!" David shook his head vigorously, "We need it at the school. My parents said it was the reason for the school, or something like that. My great-grandfather brought it from Europe. And Mel said it had something to do with the school's destiny."

"David, I'm sorry, I really am, but you don't understand. We can't get it back." She stretched out her arm toward David. "It was used for the bail! Just leave it alone David." Miss Hansen turned her back and walked toward her desk.

"I can't leave it alone!" David shouted. Feeling angry and helpless, he stormed out.

CHAPTER TWENTY-SIX
TAKING CHANCES

David had a sleepless night. He needed to get that business card from Miss Hansen. Grabbing his coat and flashlight, he crept out of his room.

When he got to the school building, he heard Mel working in the boiler room. Loud worship music played, and Mel had his back to the door. David remembered something from his time working with Mel: Mel always put his keychain on his desk when he wasn't using it. Sure enough, it was there on the desk to the right of the door. David slipped in and took the keys.

He tried to sneak upstairs, but it was SO dark. He didn't want to use his flashlight because Mel would notice it. The darkness took his breath away and he tried to concentrate on his mission. His knees knocked. A bright light from above blinded him.

David jumped. "Need some help?" a voice called out from behind the light. The flashlight changed its focus, and David saw JJ and Julia standing on the stairway in their pajamas.

"How did you know what I was doing?" he

called up to them.

"We followed you," laughed Julia, "Say hello to Nancy Drew and Sherlock Holmes!"

David wanted to hug them. In fact, he did, right there on the landing of the school stairs!

"Let's hurry," said Julia.

"Let's get this over with." JJ yawned.

With the help of the strong flashlights, the kids were able to get up to Classroom 7.

JJ handed David a smaller flashlight that fit into the palm of his hand. He went right to

Miss Hansen's desk and tugged on the middle drawer. The old wooden drawer groaned as he

opened it. Almost immediately, he found the card for the glass shop.

"Got it" He grinned as he held the card up in front of the small light.

The next morning, David felt guilty about sneaking into Miss Hansen's desk, and decided to, at least, return the keys. He had to do the right thing. David was still determined to get the star back, since it was important to his family, the school and even the men he had seen when he was with Evod, but he didn't want to start on a path of stealing things.

David forced himself to trudge into the boiler room. He dropped the keys on Mel's table.

Mel looked up from the book he was reading. "How did you get these? I looked all over for them. Good thing I have a second set."

David decided to tell the truth, but not the WHOLE truth.

"I'm sorry, Mel. I needed them last night."

Instead of giving David a lecture, Mel just looked

at him. He seemed to be scanning David's face for a lie. Now it was David's turn to look into Mel's eyes. He saw a twinkle there.

Mel sighed. "David, do the right thing. But be careful. And stay close to Evod."

"You know what I'm thinking?"

"Yes, you're thinking you have to get the star back. I agree. I can't help you now, but the dove can."

David shifted his weight uneasily and adjusted the backpack straps on his shoulders.

It felt so empty now without the star. "Okay, Mel, I'll do it – get the star back somehow."

Mel smiled. "You already have a plan. Like I said, stay close to Evod. He knows the way."

David hardly slept that night either. As the sun rose, his mind was made up.

He reached under his bed and picked up the business card for the glass shop. He read it over and over. He saw a picture of the Dove in his mind. At that very moment, there was a tapping at his window. *Evod!*

Filled with courage, he dressed quickly and hid in his room until all the students had left for class. He was skipping school! The first time ever! He hoped it will be the last. His heart felt like it was going to beat out of his chest. After all the noises died down, he looked out the window. There was Evod again.

David knew if he followed him, he would be okay because Evod always protected him and Julia. Even Mel knew that, he said so yesterday!

David ran all the way to town on the back roads.

He found the glass shop easily by following Evod. He bolted through the door. Gulping for air, he burst out "I've come for the glass star my teacher, Miss Hansen, sold you."

The smiling lady behind the counter said, "We sold it to Mr. Strumpstein –you know, that very rich man."

"Mr. Strumpstein? Uh, do you know where he lives?" David could hardly speak, because he was out of breath, and now there was a huge lump in his throat.

"No, but he's very famous, you could probably find him online, or on one of those Twitter things."

David laughed inside; she didn't know anything about technology! But his thoughts turned to anger and disappointment. The star wasn't there!

The old lady looked at him closely, sensing his disappointment. "I'm sorry, dear. He paid a lot of money for it- you probably won't be able to get it back. But if it means that much to you, I hope you do."

David leaned against the counter. At least he did have a name, a place to start. Maybe Julia could help him come up with a plan. His shoulders drooped. He should have told her he was coming here. "I've got to get back now," he told the lady and dashed out the door.

Evod led the way again, and David's feet barely touched the pavement. He'd better hurry. They'll come looking for him after attendance is taken! David snuck in the back door of the dorm. When he got to his room, he stuffed blankets under his door, and hid in his bed until he knew school would be over. It looked like he got away with not showing up, at least for now. He looked up Mr. Strumpstein's address and plotted a way to get to the man's fancy townhouse.

Finally, he heard voices. He jumped up, moved the blankets, and hid in his closet while his roommates came in, and after what seemed like forever, they left again. David crept out into the empty hallway and started out. He didn't see Evod, nor did he run into anyone as he snuck out of the building and over to Julia's dorm. No one saw him or asked any questions. It was great, but unexplainable, kind of like when they had returned from their first adventure with the dove.

Fortunately, Julia was just coming outside. He waved to her and pointed to the soccer field.

"Julia, I went to the shop and they sold it."

"You went to the glass shop? Without me?" Julia dropped her backpack and stared at him. "I wondered why you weren't in class. Miss Hansen chose me to take the attendance slip to the office, and, oops-" she giggled, "I didn't. I figured you were up to something after last night." She climbed up the bleachers and sat down.

"Yeah, I used the card and followed Evod."

"You did?"

"Yeah, I couldn't tell you because then you and JJ would get in trouble. And it looks like that was a good plan after all." David climbed up beside his friend. "Thanks for covering for me…but…the star is gone, sold!"

"Oh, David, that's awful." Julia hid her face in her hands. After a few seconds, she looked up and said, "What now?"

David was glad Julia didn't say, "let's give up, all is lost!" He said bravely, "We go visit Mr. Strumpstein."

"THE Mr. Strumpstein? He's the one who has it?" Julia stared at David.

"Yes, I'm afraid so." David played with the strap of his backpack.

"Why afraid? We can get in to see him!" Julia sat up straight, a look of excitement on her face. "I'm my father's daughter, aren't I? I told you how my dad taught me how to get what I want? (A cat with the best talent for survival?)

They both laughed. "We can figure out a way to get in to see him."

David smiled. *I'm so glad I met this girl!*

Meanwhile, the police were able to trace fingerprints found on the bomb fragments.

They led back to a known criminal. That very man had signed the school guest book the day the bomb had gone off. The suspect was immediately called in for questioning. He gave the names of his accomplices in the crime.

A group of people had planned the bombing. The police learned that they were terrorists and had bombed The American School because they didn't want anyone to study America, the cross or the star. Upon learning these facts, the police knew they had to call the FBI. The FBI took over the investigation from there.

As David and the others suspected, Mr. Aark had been at the American School for a different reason. He wanted to give the star to the principal in exchange for the money owed Naples Christian Academy. Now, Mr. Aark was cleared!

CHAPTER TWENTY-SEVEN
JEWELS

As Julia walked David home to his dorm, she saw Evod again. "Look David, Evod!"

The dove swooped in front of them and called "Follow me! Follow me!" They began to run.

"We must be on the right track, Julia. Mel said to follow the Dove and I have been," David managed.

Julia agreed. "We have to keep following him. She and David followed Evod into the basement again.

The fire appeared in the middle of the room, but it didn't consume the floor.

"The fire!" they both said at once.

The atmosphere was so overwhelming. She felt peace, love and fear all at the same time!

Julia looked down and gasped. She was covered from neck to feet with a beautiful white robe. Attached to her robe were the most stunning jewels she had ever seen. Julia looked at David. He was dressed the same way. Words burst out of her like a flood.

"Look at us, David!" she called to him. "We're covered in jewels!"

Her face shone pure joy.

David said, "Now I'm glad we didn't choose the treasure chest in that creepy field.

These jewels are three times the size of those jewels."

"Me too," replied Julia. She looked up at Evod who now hovered above her. The dove's eyes locked on hers and then seemed to scan her robe. She looked down at it. On the robe, there was a large purple stone, larger than the others. On it was carved the word "Jewel". David was staring at the jewel too.

Evod said, "You need to be protected, like a Jewel.... but you haven't been,"

"I don't feel like I deserve this robe," Julia said to Evod. I'm a nobody. I don't deserve this expensive robe, I'm a mess of a kid."

"You are loved" Evod said.

Just as she was receiving that thought, Julia saw the fire, the bird, and the robes all Disappear. She was back in the school basement. They were surrounded by the same clutter of books, old furniture, and dust. Just as before. Except for one thing.

The floor glistened.

"The jewels!" Julia called out.

Sure enough, there were six glowing stones of different colors – yellow, blue, red, orange, purple and green in the middle of the floor.

Julia knelt and scooped them up. "Do you think they are real?"

"I don't know, but this proves this is not all a

freaky bad dream. It all really happened.

"Now we have proof of our adventures."

"Let's each take three, but don't tell anybody!!" Julia said excitedly. She stuck the purple, green and red stones into her pockets.

"Now this is REALLY stealing," David warned. "This could mean big trouble."

CHAPTER TWENTY-EIGHT
JULIA'S MOM

Julia was surprised when she went home for the weekend and her mother said, "Your dad is in town. And he wants to see you."

"Here? Where?" Julia looked around the room and then at her mother.

Mom had a pained expression on her face. "Well, he's staying at that fancy motel up on Clark Street. You, know, the one on the hill with all the lights. He wants to pick you up and take you out to dinner." Julia's mother crossed her arms and swayed slightly. She looked stressed.

"Do you want to see him?"

"It's been four years! Of course, Mom." Julia sat down on the couch.

"Well, I don't want you to get hurt, after the last time."

"Oh, that was then, Mom. I'm older now. I know how Dad is. I won't get hurt." Julia shook her head firmly, feeling her long hair swish across her back.

"Well, okay. He told me on the phone he's now making lots of money and is more reliable."

Julia's mother looked down at her hands as she said, "He will take you to an actual restaurant this time. He promised no more stealing. He promised he wouldn't do anything illegal, with you along, like what led to him being arrested in front of you last time."

Julia moaned. "Oh, Mom, that was a long time ago!"

Mom's lips tightened. "I know, but take my cell phone, just in case, Julia."

"Okay, Mom. But don't worry." Julia jumped up. She took the phone and headed to her room with her suitcase. "I won't need it. I can handle Dad," she called over her shoulder.

Excited, Julia began unpacking. As she unloaded her clothes out of her suitcase,

something dropped to the floor. It was the purple jewel that said JEWEL! It had fallen from the pocket of her jeans! She scooped it up. Panic struck her. If anyone saw this, they would take it away. No! She wouldn't let them! It was hers!

Where could she hide it? She put the purple stone in her jewelry box. There was a sudden loud knock on the front door. *Dad!* The other jewels were forgotten, and Julia went off to spend time with her father.

Julia melted into her father's hug. It had been a long time, over four years since she had seen him. The last time she saw him he sat in a police squad car, picked up over writing bad checks. Julia wanted to love him, and be glad they were together again, but her mind was divided.

Julia stiffened as they walked into the dining room. Had Dad really changed?

Soft piano music wafted thru the air to Julia's ears. Candles in low glass jars lit the room. A white tablecloth covered the table the hostess led them to, and mint green napkins folded into crisp triangles served as decorations. The silverware encircling her plate glimmered in the candlelight.

Julia's father pulled her chair out for her, and waited for her to be seated before he gently scooted her under the table.

"You know, Julia. I can really provide everything you need now. Don't worry about anything. I went by the school today and talked to the principal." Julia's stomach flipped.

Dad went on. "I think he was very impressed. I told him, I have lots of money now." He smiled as he picked up his menu. "They'd better treat you right. And just to make sure, I'm going to donate to the Building Fund." He winked at her.

"Oh, no, Dad, you don't have to do that." She smiled wanly.

"But of course, I do. That's how you get ahead in this world. And I want my little girl to get ahead." He reached over and touched her under the chin.

Julia tried not to cringe. She loved her dad, but maybe Mom was right not to trust him.

Then she had another awful thought. Had Mr. Aark told him about the basement and the detention?

Dad didn't mention anything about the detention and the rest of the dinner remained uneventful, but when it was time to pay, she held her breath as the waiter took Dad's plastic card.

This is it. The moment of truth. She could always wash dishes if Dad didn't have the money. Isn't that what happened to people who didn't pay their bill? That's what Grandma told her. Julia chuckled out loud. At least she could laugh about it now.

Finally, the waiter came back with the credit card receipt and said, "Everything's taken care of, Sir. Thank you very much. Have a nice evening.

Air whooshed from her lungs, maybe Dad had changed.

When she arrived home, it was late. She opened the door quietly so she wouldn't wake her mother, but she found Mom in the living room.

"Hi Mom." Julia's mother silently stared at her hands. Julia sensed it was something important.

"Mom?" Julia walked slowly toward the couch, holding her breath.

"Julia, what are these?" The green and red jewels sparkled in her palms.

"Oh, um, something I found at school." Julia looked at her feet.

"Found at school? Julia, these gems are worth a lot of money." She looked up at Julia,

with a puzzled look on her face. "They must belong to someone."

"No, I just found them on the floor at school."

Concern reflected in her mother's eyes. "At school, where?"

"In the basement." Julia studied the cracks in their wood floor.

"The basement! What were you doing down there?" Julia could feel her mother's eyes penetrating her chest.

"I was exploring with my friend, doing research."
Julia ventured another look at her mother.

Her face was taut with concern. "Did your
teacher know you were down there?" Mom was not
going to give up.

Julia bit the inside of her lip. Should she tell the
truth, even though she'd promised David? "Oh
Yeah," Julia said and looked to the floor again.

"Well, this isn't okay, Julia. Someone is missing
these. You need to give them to Miss Hansen." Mom
gathered the jewels into one hand and stretched out
her arm to give them to Julia. She abruptly looked
up.

"With a friend, Huh?" She smiled. "I'm happy
to hear you're making friends. What's her name?"

"David."

"David? Oh, I thought it was… Well, I'm glad
you at least have a friend at school."

Mom said quietly and leaned back into the couch.

Julia took the jewels and boldness came over
her. "And we found a glass star too!"

"A glass star? Hmm. You'd better turn that in
too." Mom shook her head. Suddenly she changed
the subject. "By the way, how was your date with
your dad?"

"It was great." Julia realized she didn't want to
go any further on the subject of the star either.

"Great?" Mom cocked her head and looked at
Julia's face intently. "Anything I need to know
about?"

Julia decided to say as little as possible. "No
Mom. Dad is great. I'm tired, I'll tell you more
tomorrow."

Her mother smiled. "Okay, sweetie. Now, make sure you turn those things in

to Lost and Found or your teacher. I won't have any more larceny in this family, Ms. Hingle!"

With that, she winked and held out her arms to embrace Julia with that hug that always made Julia feel safe.

CHAPTER TWENTY-NINE
JULIA, DAVID AND... MR. AARK?

"David, you'll never guess what happened!" Julia approached David during recess.

David stopped walking towards her and froze in mock terror. "What?"

"My dad came to town and took me out to dinner. He said he talked to Mr. Aark, and they are now friends!" She looked at David's doubtful expression and said, "Don't you see, David? Maybe now Mr. Aark will not be so mean to us, to you!"

"I doubt it, Julia. Didn't you hear what he said to Mrs. Barrey when we were with Evod?

"I know, David. But this is about money! Remember Evod said Mr. Aark only cared about money?" David nodded, looking skeptical. "Well, this is about money! My dad has lots of it now, and he's going to give it to the school. Then Mr. Aark and Dorm Master Robbins and all the rest of them will treat us special, or at least better than they do now."

David shook his head. "I don't know about that, Julia."

"It will make a difference, you'll see!" Julia

smiled and skipped off down the hall towards the stairs to the classroom.

To his surprise, David discovered that what Julia predicted happened just a few days later.

At the end of the morning on Friday, the intercom came on and Mrs. Barrey asked Miss Hansen to send Julia to the office. Julia looked at David. They each lifted their eyebrows in surprise.

Julia left and about ten minutes later, the intercom interrupted class again. "Miss Hansen, will you send David to the office?"

David's stomach flipped and the muscles in his neck tightened as he trudged down the stairs and over to the Administration Department. Was he in trouble again?

Julia stood next to Mr. Aark, they both smiled.

"David," said Mr. Aark. "I have decided to start taking worthy students out to lunch with me once a month. This month, I have picked Julia Hingle, and she can bring a friend." He looked down at Julia admiringly. "Julia has picked you, David. We are going to go to Big Burgers for a treat."

David was astonished. He looked at Julia who nodded. "Sure, Mr. Aark. Thank you," was all David could say.

The chauffeured limousine that Mr. Aark often traveled in picked them up at the front door.

The children didn't say much. David still felt afraid of Mr. Aark. For his part, Mr. Aark asked Julia lots of questions about her father, like what kind of businesses he owned, and for how long. He asked her how long her father would be in town, and Julia said she didn't know. After all the questions about her father were exhausted, Mr. Aark seemed to revert to his creepy, cold self again.

When the students returned to class, a little late after lunch, they were greeted with dirty looks.

One of the girls said, "What makes you so special, Julia? We heard you and David went out to eat with Mr. Aark." Julia shrugged and looked over at David.

JJ nudged David in the ribs. "Hey, I heard Aark picked you because your family owns the school. What gives?"

"Nothing, JJ." David shook his head. "He said it was a new program where he picks kids to go out to lunch each month." David looked at Julia. "It was just Julia's turn this month."

David didn't believe this was a new program, and it seemed the other students didn't either. They were proved correct when the next month came and went and no students were picked to go out to lunch with Mr. Aark.

Julia's father left town the next month.

"David, he didn't even say goodbye!" Julia sobbed through tears, as David tried to console her the afternoon she found out from her mother.

David didn't know how to comfort his friend. He reached out and put his hand on her elbow.

"Well, Julia. That probably means he intends to be right back. You don't need to worry about it."

They walked into the classroom and everyone's eyes were on Julia. This just made her cry more. After a few minutes, Miss Hansen stopped the lesson she was teaching. "Julia dear, would you like to be excused from the room? Perhaps go see your mother?"

Julia nodded.

Miss Hansen went to her desk, scribbled something and handed Julia a slip of paper.

Julia jumped up quickly and ran out the door. David followed his friend with his eyes. He wished he could go with her to make sure she was alright.

Later, at dinner, David saw Julia. He strode toward her. "Are you feeling better?"

"No, I'm not." Anger burned in her eyes. "It turns out my dad didn't just desert me again. He deserted the school too!"

"What do you mean?"

"Well, when I went to see my mom, she was so angry, livid. I guess you'd say using our last vocabulary word."

"Angry-why?" David asked softly as they carried their trays to their table.

"Well, it seems my dad gave Mr. Aark a check for the school. Remember, that's why Mr. Aark was so nice and took us out to lunch?"

"I sure do," David said as they sat down.

"Well, it turns out that my dad's check was no good. He didn't give ANY money to the school!"

"What? How awful." David looked around. "What did Mr. Aark say?"

"I didn't see him, David, but I guess he was furious about it." She lowered her voice. "And he seemed to blame my mom. He wants her to pay him the money now! I just started crying. Mom took me on her lap and we both cried. Mom was right. I shouldn't have trusted my dad again." Julia sobbed quietly.

"That's terrible," David said. For the rest of dinner neither of them spoke.

Poor Julia, David thought. *How awful it must be to have a father like that!*

David wanted to tell her "It must be awful to have a father like that! My dad always tells the truth," but he thought better of it.

CHAPTER THIRTY
JULIA IN TROUBLE

The next Monday, David was surprised to see that Julia wasn't in class. He asked her roommates where she was, and they said her mother had come to their room the night before. After the girls came back from basketball practice, they noticed Julia and her suitcase were gone.

David's heart ached. She left school without telling him? What could have happened? Was she ok? When David didn't see Julia turn up in the next two days, he asked Miss Hansen.

"Julia?" Miss Hansen looked surprised. "Julia? Oh, I'm sure she's fine. Don't worry about it, David, but if you are that concerned, I can check with Mrs. Hingle in the office.

Why didn't he think of that?

After school, David headed to Mrs. Hingle's office. As he turned the corner leading to her cubicle, he heard yelling. "Is this retaliation for my ex-husband? Because this is not fair." Mrs. Hingle faced Mrs. Barrey. Both women were white-faced and looked very angry.

"Delia, Mrs. Hingle, Mr. Aark made it very clear

to me. Since you were not an employee of the school when you enrolled Julia, her tuition is not free."

"That's ridiculous! The whole reason I enrolled Julia is because you promised her tuition would be free!" Mrs. Hingle looked down at a paper in her hand. "And then I get this- I owe twelve thousand dollars!" She slapped the paper with her opposite hand. "You know full well I don't have twelve thousand dollars! I can't afford to pay that for Julia to stay here!"

David ducked behind the corner. Now he knew why Julia wasn't in school.

Poor Julia! Poor Mrs. Hingle! What are they going to do?

David wanted more than anything to find out where Julia was. Was she hiding at her mother's house? Was she with her father? He thought about all these possibilities, but he was afraid to talk to the grownups while they were so upset. It was a long week for David, waiting and wondering about Julia.

That weekend, David received the happy surprise answer to where Julia was.

He walked into his home, and there she was seated in David's living room.

"Julia," David rushed up to her and hugged her tight. "What are you doing here?"

"My mom brought me, David." Julia sat down. "She found out that the school doesn't want me to go there anymore because we don't have the money. Mom wants to continue working, but I can't stay in the dorm."

"But why here, Julia?"

Julia smiled. "Mom found out that your mother

is on the board of the school that makes the decisions. She brought me here and talked to your mom about the problem." Julia sighed. "Your mom is so nice, David! She made me cookies and said I could stay here until the trouble was over."

"Thank God for my mom!" David exclaimed. He looked up into the kitchen doorway and saw his mother standing there. He rushed into her arms. "Thank you, thank you."

That night, David's parents sat down at the table and explained about the star to David and Julia. "You see, kids." David's father began. "The star brings together the Children of the Star, and the Children of the Cross."

"Mel said that!" David piped up.

His mother smiled. "Yes, Mel would know that. He knows about a book my grandfather wrote too."

"He gave us the book, Mom."

"He gave it to you?" Mrs. Roth looked surprised. "Well, then you've read it."

"Some of it," said David. "Enough to know how the school started, and what great-grandfather Moishe believed."

David's father interrupted. "The important thing is, without the star there would be no cross. The star came first. And that's what was so special about the school. It used to teach about both the star and the cross."

"Wow" said David. "I wish I had been there then."

"Me too," said Julia.

The next day, she told David. "David, in my

dream I saw a tree. It started to talk to me. Then I saw many trees. I realized they were the trees around your house."

David grinned and looked out the window as they sat in the living room.

"The trees spoke to me about the kindness I felt from your family." She looked around the room. "I feel such love and peace here, too. And it has something to do with the star."

"I know it does, "said David. "Anything more?"

"Oh, yes," said Julia. "In the next dream, I saw myself standing in front of the star. It was bigger, as tall as I am. The wind blew my hair, and then the wind whipped around me and my whole body was shaking. But I was not afraid."

"Cool," whispered David.

"Yeah, it was awesome. I sang a beautiful song like the song the men were singing, and I got taller and taller."

"Wow, that's amazing!" David moved closer to Julia. "What do you think it means?"

"I think I know what it means, David…I'm going to stay at the school and continue fighting to learn about the star with you." She lifted her chin and David thought she looked very brave.

CHAPTER THIRTY-ONE
DAVID'S MOTHER TO THE RESCUE

David's mother received an important phone call that weekend. She was told about an emergency meeting of the Naples Christian Academy's School Board. Since her family had started the school, Lily Roth was a lifetime member of the Board and she was required to attend and vote.

Lily didn't mind going. She intended to appeal to the Board to re-admit Julia. The following Wednesday, she stopped at David's dorm.

"I'm on my way to that board meeting, David."

"I want to go with you, Mom"

"Now David," she said, "I've been to these meetings many times before. Sometimes it is just three hours of complaining."

"Yes, Mom, but," David looked up at his mother and suddenly felt very mature. "I want to see what will happen about Julia."

Lily and David showed up on the rainy evening, with Lily having no expectations of the meeting being short. She shook the rain off her umbrella as they entered the school building. "Are you sure you are going to be able to sit through this?

"Yes." Their eyes met and they both smiled.

Inside the musty downstairs meeting room, a sour-faced woman pounded a gavel and called the meeting to order. David took a seat behind his mother, who sat at a large table. The adults went through the Secretary's Report, Treasurers Report, and Old Business. Mrs. Barrey called out in a loud voice, "And now the New Business: Permanent Expulsion of Julia Hingle." The crowd gasped. David cried out. Lily put her hand on David's arm to quiet him.

"Why would they do such a thing to such a sweet little girl?" whispered the lady in the front row to the woman beside her.

Lily raised her hand. "Madame Chairman, may I ask a question? Why is this item on our agenda?"

The lady scowled. "The reason is her tuition has not been paid. She was enrolled before her mother worked at the school. So, her tuition is not free as it is for other staff's children."

Mrs. Barrey looked around the room with a haughty smile. "They owe us quite a bit of money. Besides, her father made a pledge to the school, and his check bounced. We do not fund charity cases here at Naples Christian Academy".

One board member spoke up. "I object!" said a grey-haired lady in a blue suit.

"Mrs. Hingle is an invaluable member of our staff. We cannot afford to lose her. Julia should attend for free."

"I agree," said a tall man in a dark suit. "The child should not be made to suffer for the mistakes of her parent….and the administration." He glared at Mrs.

Barrey and Mr. Aark.

This man looked familiar to David. Was he the man that was on TV the day of the explosion, Mr. Strumpstein?

There was a lot a mumbling and disagreement as a lengthy discussion followed. David

tried to say something too, but Mom shook her head and mouthed the word "No."

David knew better than to disobey his mother. His head begin to ache, and he sank down under the table.

It seemed like forever before Mrs. Roth raised her hand. "This is not fair. We obviously do not have all the facts." Lily looked down at David as she said, "I move that we postpone the vote until we can look over all the information. We need at least a month to make a decision."

The motion was seconded and everyone on the Board voted to postpone the decision.

David's stomach and head calmed, but now he was exhausted. He looked to his mom for some comfort, but she was busy talking to the other Board Members.

Finally, the meeting was adjourned. Mr. Aark and Mrs. Barrey stormed out of the room. They did not look happy.

A wave of relief swept over David. He stood up and hugged his mother. "Now to tell Julia," he said.

When they got home, they found that Julia's mother had come to the house. David excitedly told her, Julia and his father what had happened.

Delia leaned over her daughter, brushed a stray hair out of her eyes, and said, "You'd better stay here a little while longer, Honey. I can't leave you home alone, and the Roths have been kind enough to say you can stay here during the day. David can bring your schoolwork here on the weekends so you can stay caught up." She sighed and shook her head. "I'm afraid, I'm under too much scrutiny to take time off, and you might be bothered if you tried to come to the school."

David's mother drove him back to school. Before she dropped him off at the dorm, she and David went to Mel's office. He smiled and stood up when they entered.

Mrs. Roth told Mel all that had happened at the meeting. "I'm not surprised," said Mel.

"Mr. Aark and Mrs. Barrey always have something up their sleeves. Something evil and something against the star."

"I'm sure you're right, Mel." Mrs. Roth adjusted her coat. "Now, could you help me locate the material- the paperwork- that tells the qualifications for free tuition? And even

how my vote affects the votes of the School Board?"

"Sure thing, Mrs. R." Mel winked at David. He didn't seem worried at all about Julia and what was going on with her. Mel and David's mother met every night for weeks to comb through the old records of the school. They went into the basement, and David and Julia went with them.

David hoped the fire, or Evod would show up, so the grownups would see. It didn't happen.

Finally, after three weeks, Mel found the papers they were looking for. He pulled them out of the old filing cabinet where David and Julia had found the star.

"Here it is!" Mel held the paper above his head and laughed. "But how did it get- oh never mind." He lowered the paper and read. "Voting requirements. IN case of a tie, an heir of Moishe Blum- that's you, Mrs. R. is required to vote and break the tie."

"Yay!" David lept into the air.

Julia jumped up and down.

"This is great, just what we were looking for." David's mom looked close to tears. Armed with the new information, they triumphantly walked David back to his dorm.

At the meeting one week later, Julia and her mother accompanied Lily and David. As they walked into the meeting room, David grabbed an agenda off the table.

"There you are, Julia...reinstatement."

"It could be they are reinstating someone else." Mrs. Hingle looked worried.

"No, it says Vote." David looked up at his mom.

"I'm pretty sure that's the vote for Julia, Delia." Lily's voice was soft and calming.

David's stomach was full of butterflies, as the Board voted. The happy result was that she was put back in Naples Christian Academy.

The next day, the Roths drove Julia to the school. She got nasty stares as she moved back into her dorm, and even in class for a few days, but she kept going with her head held high.

"I'm so glad you're back in school, Julia." David said the first day afterschool when they were alone. David felt bashful as he looked down and mumbled.

"I missed you."

Julia didn't seem embarrassed. "I missed you too." She gave him a hug. "Now we know a lot more about the power of the star. Lots of people want to hear about it, but lots of people have something against it. We'll have to be careful, David."

"I was thinking the same thing. We'll have to keep our talks even more secret." He looked around. "I sure hope Evod shows up soon. We MUST get the star back into the school. We just have to!"

CHAPTER THIRTY-TWO
TREASURE HUNT

"There are a couple of trucks in this parking lot here," said JJ. "Which one do we use?"

"I don't know," said Julia as she scanned the list in her hand. "The treasure hunt list just said a truck."

"Why did Miss Hansen send us on the treasure hunt anyway? Doesn't she remember all the rules since the 'war' began?" David frowned. "I wonder if she is still mad at me for yelling at her, and she wants to catch me doing something wrong."

"Stop worrying, David." Julia scolded. "This is fun. Just enjoy yourself for once." Julia and JJ laughed.

"How about that one over there?" Julia pointed to a white truck.

"I don't believe it," David yelled. "Do you see what's printed on the side? Strumpstein Construction! Someone here has a connection with Mr. Strumpstein!"

"You're right, David! But who could it be?" Julia asked.

Just then, Mel walked out from within the cluster of buildings and opened the door to the cab of the white truck.

"Mel!" yelled David. He took off running, and the other two followed. "Mel, is that your truck?"

Mel turned towards the children. "Yes, what are you three doing here?" Mel stepped back and waited for all three to get to him.

"We're on a treasure hunt for Miss Hansen." Julia panted.

"A treasure hunt?" He chuckled. "Seems like you kids are always on some sort of a treasure hunt." They all chuckled and nodded their heads.

"And we found a treasure. Your truck!" David pointed with an open hand.

Mel shook his head. "Haha, I don't see how this old truck could be a treasure! You must be dreaming."

"We are dreaming, IN A GOOD WAY." Julia laughed. "Well, maybe.... Mel, why does your truck say Strumpstein Construction?"

"Oh, because sometimes I work for Strumpstein Construction on the weekends, when I'm not here at school."

"Really?" David and Julia stared at each other.

"Yes, really. Why do you ask?"

Julia stepped up to Mel. "Mel, do you know Mr. Strumpstein? Do you think you could take us to meet him?"

Mel said, "Sure, anytime. Mr. Strumpstein is really nice. I go to his house all the time."

"Next Saturday?" Julia pressed in.

"Well, I guess so. But we'd have to get permission from your folks." Mel swung his leg into the truck.

"Permission will be granted," Julia said firmly as she grinned at David and JJ.

CHAPTER THIRTY-THREE
MR. STRUMPSTEIN

Neither David nor Julia slept much Friday night. They stayed at the dorm so it would be easier for Mel to round them up and take them over to Mr. Strumpstein's

Castle. JJ came along, but he didn't know this meeting was going to be about the star. As they climbed into the truck, the three kids took a deep breath. Mel looked across the truck seat at them. "Relax, there's nothing to be afraid of. Mr. Strumpstein is very nice. Just remember your manners." He started the truck, and they were on their way.

Mel introduced David, Julia and JJ to Mr. Strumpstein at the door. They shook hands with the distinguished gentlemen in the grey suit.

"Come in, come in," he said with a smile. "Would you like something to eat? I had my people prepare a little something." He motioned into the luxurious living room.

David turned to the room and saw a centerpiece that looked like a Christmas tree, and was almost as tall. The kids gasped. Porcelain plates hung from each branch. Each plate held either a cupcake, doughnut, or stack of cookies.

"Don't mind if I do." JJ walked directly to the tree. David and Julia were too nervous to eat. Besides, they didn't want to eat his food before they had a chance to ask him about the star. He might not be too happy about being asked to give up one of his possessions.

Then David saw it on top of the huge ornate piano! David nudged Julia who nodded and let out a cry.

"What's the matter. Are you ok? Eat, eat." Mr. Strumpstein was seated now.

So was JJ. He had three plates on his lap and was stuffing his mouth.

"Uh, we're not hungry," Julia said looking at David. She flicked her shoulder at him, "Are we, David?"

"Oh, no, no. We had a big breakfast."

Mel stared at them and then turned toward Mr. Strumpstein. He hadn't noticed the star.

Mel and Mr. Strumpstein made small talk. They discussed the weather and the school and then began talking about how Mel was doing on the Strumpstein projects.

David could stand it no longer. "Mr. Strumpstein, where did you get the star?"

"Oh," Mr. Strumpstein looked up. "I acquired that recently. A wonderful find. In a quaint little shop in town. Got it for a great price!" He sat back, beaming.

"Well, it is beautiful, but I would have you know it is an old artifact from World War II. It belonged to my grandfather and great-grandfather and it was given to our school.

We would like it back."

Mr. Strumpstein was silent. So were Mel and JJ.

Julia tried to fix the conversation. "What he means to say, Mr. Strumpstein, is we admire the star. We feel it should be at the school. Maybe we could work out something." She walked over to the older man and continued softly. "The school needs it. You want people to think that you are a nice man, don't you? Maybe you could donate it back to the school."

"Donate? Why, that star is worth a lot of money! Why can't the school buy it back?

Why did they sell it in the first place?" Mr. Strumpstein's face turned red.

"We had to sell it to pay for Mr. Aark to get out of jail.," David said.

"Really?" Mr. Strumpstein's eyebrows went up. There was a deep silence. Then he spoke. "Kids, I understand what you're saying. But I'd really have to think about it. My wife and I love the star. We think it looks great right here in our home." He gestured around the living room. "And we will take good care of it."

David's heart broke. He tried not to cry in front of everyone. "Well, Mr. Strumpstein,

would you at least think about it? You could call the school. The Board. My mother is on the School Board. Maybe you two could work something out. Please?"

"Ok, I will…er, think about it." Mr. Strumpstein stood up.

Mel's voice was very calm. "Of course, you will,

Mr. Strumpstein. Now we'd better get going. Thank you for your time." Mel motioned to the children and they moved towards the door to leave.

"Wait, don't go yet. Take some of these snacks." Mr. Strumpstein turned and called into another room, "Letty, please pack up the treats so the children can take them back to school."

A maid in a white uniform instantly appeared. She carried small white boxes and removed the cookies, cupcakes and doughnuts and put them into the boxes.

Mr. Strumpstein seemed hurried now. "I must excuse myself. Thank you all for coming. It was a pleasure meeting you, children." He shook hands with each of them. When he got to David, David looked up into his eyes. It looked like Mr. Strumpstein was about to cry!

He turned away quickly. "I'd better go now. Goodbye! Take your time, take all the treats you want," he called over his shoulder.

Mel shrugged. "And that, kids was Mr. Strumpstein. He sure seemed upset at the end.

Looked like he was going to cry." Mel shook his head. "I've never seen him like that before."

"I hope he's not upset because of YOU, David," JJ said with his mouth still full. He gave David a nasty look. David just looked down.

Julia spoke up in his defense. "David was just telling the truth."

The boxes were ready, and Mel loaded them and the children into the truck.

"What a strange meeting," JJ said after they were seated. They all nodded in agreement.

CHAPTER THIRTY-FOUR
"KEEP YOUR EYES OPEN"

The truck was silent as Mel drove the children back to Naples Christian Academy.

No one spoke, and no one dared to. A heaviness fell over the foursome, and David replayed the meeting in his head. Why had he said all those things? He'd been wrong to do so and now worry clenched his stomach. Would Mr. Strumpstein help them?

"I'm disappointed that Mr. Strumpstein is so against helping us." Julia turned to Mel. "We're just kids! And it's our star and our school. You'd think he would be more generous!"

Mel said nothing.

"I only ate a little bit, and then we had to go, and now I have to share the food with the whole school! David, you and Julia are getting all worked up over nothing. Sure, the star was magic, but so what?" JJ turned his body to face them both. "Mr. Strumpstein has a right to it, he BOUGHT it. And if it really belongs at the school, it will get back there somehow.

After all it is magic, right?"

Mel nodded and smiled. A huge rainbow appeared across the road up ahead. Before Mel drove through it, Evod swept down and flew through the gigantic arch.

"Wow!! Hey, did you see that?" exclaimed JJ. It was the first time he had seen Evod.

"That huge bird, what was that? And it seemed so peaceful!"

David said, "It was Evod! He's our friend, Julia and mine. I'm so glad he showed up again. He can help us. Right, Julia?"

Julia looked up, emerging from her daze of depression. "Evod came?"

Mel chuckled, "Yes, he did. We saw him, Julia. You'll never know what you'll see when you keep your eyes open."

CHAPTER THIRTY-FIVE
ANOTHER STRANGE MEETING

"Will Julia Hingle, David Roth and James Jones come to the office, please?" Mrs. Barrey said through the intercom the following Monday morning.

David stood and walked out the door with Julia and JJ. He walked to Mr. Aark's office in a daze. When he opened the door, he was shocked to see his parents, Mr. Aark, Miss Hansen, Julia's mother, JJ's parents, and Mel.

"I had Mrs. Barrey call all the parties involved and we decided to meet." Mr. Aark cleared his throat and glared at the children. "Now, we're all here because we adults are becoming concerned about your behavior."

David looked around at everyone. "Why?"

Mr. Aark spoke loudly. "David, you've got to give up on this star thing."

"Why?" David blinked his eyes as he looked at Mr. Aark's red face.

"Because it's not important anymore. It's old history, and it has served its purpose.

All this talk about stars, and books and jewels is

nonsense."

"Not important? Nonsense?" David looked at his mother. "Mom?"

His mom looked worried but said nothing.

"If my son is interested in this," his father said. "Only he can decide what to think about the star. Isn't that what you teach here? Thinking for yourself?"

Mr. Aark began pacing and shaking his head. "But running away, breaking into the

basement, Miss Hansen's desk, stealing things—"

Miss Hansen added, "Telling untruths, sneaking around, going places that are off-limits unsupervised—"

Julia's mother cut in. "Julia, I think it's best if you don't spend so much time with David." She looked sadly at Mrs. Roth and said, "I appreciate all you've done for us, but..."

"Mom!" shrieked Julia. "How can you say that?"

JJ jumped up. He looked at his parents. "What's wrong with David?" They said nothing.

They looked very confused and overwhelmed. This was all new information to them.

Mr. Aark ignored the last two comments and pressed on. "David, I'm glad you gave the star to Miss Hansen." He smiled at her, and then looked at David. "It helped set me free, but really, please let the adults handle things from now on."

JJs dad spoke up, "Oh, pu-leaze, just let the kids be!"

JJ walked up to his father. "Dad, Mr. Strumpstein has the star now."

Julia walked to the center of the room and scanned the faces of the adults. "I hope you're all happy. We can't get it back now."

"Yeah, JJ said. "He didn't want to give it to us."

"That is what he *said*," Mel commented from the back of the room. Everyone turned and looked at Mel. David thought *What could **that** mean?*

Mr. Aark ignored them. "David, Julia and JJ, you have earned detention, and there will be no contact with each other for two weeks."

David yelled, "No-"

Julia called out "That can't be!"

"No way", JJ said.

Mr. Aark put his hand up. "And no more talk of this star or worse consequences may result. You could all be permanently suspended from school!"

All the parents cried out, "No!"

"Think about this Julia," Julia's mom said. "This is serious!"

JJs dad growled. "Don't overreact, Aark."

A buzzer interrupted them. Then, Mrs. Barrey's voice: "Mr. Aark, there's a Mr.Stump- Strumpstein on the line."

Everyone froze. They looked at Mr. Aark. He picked up the phone. "Yes, yes, I see."

He paused. "Yes, you can come over."

A tense twenty minutes passed, as no one spoke. David's mom and Julia's mom cried softly. David and Julia paced the floor.

Finally, the door opened, and an excited Mr. Strumpstein burst in. "It's the star! The star!" He looked at David. "Young man, I have to give it back!" He looked at the others.

"A dove visited me. It wouldn't let me sleep…Or give me any rest." He walked over to David.

"Your grandfather, Aaron, was my cousin. I know about the star. Where it came from."

David's mother gasped and looked at his father.

Mr. Strumpstein walked over to her. "It's true. I kept my identity hidden. I bought the star because I knew how important it was to the Children of the Star and the Children of the Cross!" He took a deep breath. His face was purple. "But I know where it belongs now. It belongs here." He pointed to Mr. Aark's desk. Looking at Mr. Aark, he continued, "You must allow the study of the star. You must honor it. And I will donate $300,000 for the training of the teachers."

Everyone gasped. Mr. Strumpstein walked closer to the principal, who now seemed to be cowering.

"If you teach about the star, and the cross and base the school on its teachings, I will help you. I'll see to it that the school prospers and grows, and all the students are filled with knowledge and hope." He put his hand out to Mr. Aark. "Will you do it, Mr. Aark? Will you shake on it?"

Shocked and honored that such a rich and famous man would offer to partner with

him, Mr. Aark sprang to his feet. "Yes, I will, Mr. Strumpstein. Yes. I will." He shook Mr. Strumpstein's hand.

Mel snapped a quick picture. Everyone applauded. Now, David and Julia, and their mothers wept with joy.

CHAPTER THIRTY-SIX
VINDICATION AND HUMILITY

With knees trembling, David entered the
Principal's office. He scarcely breathed as his shoes
glided across the luxurious multi-toned carpet. It had
been three weeks since Mr. Strumpstein had made a
deal with the school, and Mr. Aark had summoned
David to his office. Now was the time for David to
speak the truth. He knew it in his bones, even though
they were shaking. He must speak…and tell Mr.
Aark about the importance of the star.

Mr. Aark turned, and David could tell he had
been crying. Instead of being intimidated, David
took the role of a comforter to this man thirty years
his senior.

"What's the matter, Mr. Aark?"

Mr. Aark just shook his head.

"Can you tell me what is wrong?" David asked
gently. "Is it what I have done, because…"

"No, no David," said Mr. Aark. "It's the school.
I've lost direction. I want to do what's right but…I
don't know what IS right anymore…If only…" His
voice trailed off and his gaze went down to the
desktop in a gesture of shame.

"If only what, Mr. Aark?" David blurted out, daring to believe that Mr. Aark was sorry for being so mean to the kids.

"Well, you tell me. I know you've been researching the star. Perhaps the star has the answers. Perhaps it will lead us…like the Star of Bethlehem." Mr. Aark stopped. He slowly lifted his eyes. They met David's eyes. He smiled with a half-smile. Then he looked desperate. "Tell me what this all means. I really want to hear."

David was dumbfounded. The "king" wanted to hear from the "prophet"? And this time the "king" was crying, broken, and admitting his mistakes?

Slowly and deliberately, David began to explain about the Star. As he spoke, the hair at the back of his neck and down his arms stood up. He watched Mr. Aark's face, as if in a dream. David felt slightly dizzy and very, very warm. He glanced out the window, and saw Evod outside, smiling at them.

David took a deep breath and began.

"The Jewish faith is the foundation of Christianity. There are many things that don't make sense in Christianity unless we look at Judaism. My great-grandfather knew this. When he started the school, he put a star in the foyer of the school to honor the Jewish roots of our faith. That's what Julia and I found. We also have a helper, Evod the dove. He led us to the star and my great-grandfather's book. Mel knows this too. We need to honor our Jewish ancestors. The elders in Heaven are Jewish, the writers of the New Testament are Jewish and everything sits on a Jewish foundation. It is all connected."

David felt inadequate. But the look on Mr. Aark's face made David believe he had spoken the most important words the principal had ever heard. Somehow, David felt that this meeting in Mr. Aark's office was the beginning of a new era for the school.

Evod swept in. "I know what I know and I do what I do. The adventure has just begun for the Children and for you. So where do I, Evod, lead, you ask? David was a Child of the Star seeking hope. Julia was a Child of the Cross, seeking hope too. So were all the adults.

Where does the Dove lead? The answer is I lead Home. I lead all children and grownups …

HOME.

Coming Soon: If you would like to hear more
from Evod, you can sign up for my newsletter,
Evodspeaks.
Go to my website layabrandt.com

Welcome!

Laya is a wife, mother and grandmother who lives in the Pacific Northwest. She studied acting and theater at Northwestern University in Evanston, IL before moving with her husband to Oregon to start a family. She was a stay-at home mother and co-owned a construction company for over twenty years. She was the customer contact person at the family construction company and sold Mary Kay Cosmetics. She returned to school to earn a Master's Degree in Teaching in 2003. Upon graduation, she taught in the elementary classroom for 10 years. She is currently a substitute teacher as she pursues her writing dreams. Laya is proud to be the wife of her loving husband, the mother of three grown children and a grandmother to five.

Raised in a Reformed Jewish home, she met her Messiah at the age of twenty-seven. During the past approximately forty years, she pursued an active adventure following Jesus (Yeshua) and learning His ways. The Bible has come alive to her in new ways as she's examined the linkage between the Old and

New Testaments. She also taught Sunday School and Vacation Bible School. She enjoyed imparting her love for the Lord and His Word to little children.

Over the years, she has taken the opportunity to speak at churches, retreats and parachurch organizations such as Aglow. The topics she has addressed include her personal testimony and the Jewish roots of Christianity. She often includes a Jewish dance or praise dance in her presentations. (She has led several dance troupes and taught dance to children and adults.)

She is a member of Oregon Christian Writers and the Society of Children's Book Writers and Illustrators. She studied online with Jerry Jenkins and Writing Storybooks for Children.

Made in the USA
Monee, IL
12 April 2021